THE GIRL AND THE MIDNIGHT MURDER

A.J. RIVERS

The Girl and the Midnight Murder
Copyright © 2021 by A.J. Rivers

All rights reserved. Without limiting the rights under copyright reserved above, no part of this publication may be reproduced, stored in or introduced into retrieval system, or transmitted, in any form, or by any means (electronic, mechanical, photocopying, recording, or otherwise) without the prior written permission of both the copyright owner and the above publisher of this book.

This is a work of fiction. Names, characters, places, brands, media, and incidents are either the products of the author's imagination or are used fictitiously. The author acknowledges the trademarked status and trademark owners of various products referenced in this work of fiction, which have been used without permission. The publication/use of these trademarks is not authorized, associated with, or sponsored by the trademark owners.

THE GIRL AND THE MIDNIGHT MURDER

PROLOGUE

THE FIRE ESCAPE HUNG ON THE BACK OF THE BUILDING LIKE RUSTED ivy. Years of rain and snow, of beating sun and whipping wind, had reduced it to a flaking skeleton of the promise of safety it once held. It was a strange concept, giving comfort and a sense of security by offering a means of escape from certain death.

A deep fall sunset sinking below the horizon behind the building swelled burnt orange around the edges of the cold brick. It brought to mind images of engulfing flames and suffocating heat, even in the chill drawing the day down into night.

The figure standing in ankle-high matted growth in the back lot didn't draw any attention. The coat hanging from his broad shoulders wasn't out of place and anyone would understand the hat pulled down over vulnerable ears to meet the collar lifted up to protect the sides of his neck. He could have been anyone. He was no one.

He lifted a phone to the side of his head and held it there as his eyes burrowed into each of the windows cut into the back of the building. No one could hear him speaking even if they were only a few feet away from him. The rumble of his voice was lost in the wind. It might not have existed at all.

His strides to the smooth stretch of concrete at the base of the building were confident. Familiarity wrapped a gloved hand around the bottom of the fire escape ladder and tugged it down. It resisted with a groan like it had already settled in for the evening. It didn't want to move from its chosen spot. There was no telling how many years had passed since anyone had tried to pull that ladder down to the ground.

In a way, that was reassuring. But it didn't mean much in the end.

The force of his hand brought the ladder down for a brief touch on the cement before bouncing back up to where it was meant to hang. He put his foot onto the bottom rung and launched himself up, climbing without hesitation toward the third floor. No shadows came to the windows to his right, but even if they had, he wouldn't have stopped.

It was simple, really, and yet so few people understood it. The easiest way to do anything and have no one pay attention is just to look intentional and unconcerned. He had learned long before to never look like he needed to be noticed. If it didn't seem like he should be noticed, he wouldn't be. So often details were remembered for no other reason than someone brought the attention to themselves.

Hesitating. Looking around. Tiny movements that showed discomfort or uncertainty.

Familiarity blended into nothingness. He became background scenery.

At the top of the ladder, he stepped onto the rusted fire escape and waited while it adjusted to his weight. He didn't want to risk trusting it fully, not knowing how long it had been since the escape was used. That lack of trust was really no different than anything else. He wasn't so whimsical and innocent as to make the statement that he trusted no one or that no one was deserving of trust.

It wasn't beyond him that trust existed for some. Perhaps even many. Just not for him. If it did, he couldn't do what he did. That was their reality. This was his.

The fire escape held; he stepped across it in long strides that brought him around the space of the ladder from above and approached the window. It was another lingering mark of the age of the building and the metal climbing up the back. With only a window as their means of egress, the people inside could only hope they had the chance to open it or break it if they needed to get out. And their bodies had to contort to the size and positioning of the opening in the brick to allow them out. It would be a hard ask for a good portion of adults.

For anyone without the height, weight, and flexibility within the parameters who couldn't reach the front door, the window that was meant as their way out would be nothing more than a view out into the world they were leaving behind. He could only imagine the shattering of the glass in a desperate search for the air right outside, and the backdraft it would cause as the flames fed on the new surge of oxygen.

This window wasn't broken, but it was old. The lock that once gave so many people the absolute sense that they were protected was now merely an obsolete piece of metal that needed only the right pressure and encouragement to pop open. He made quick work of it, and as the last of the sunset's glow melted into the ground, he ducked under the flaking green paint of the lifted windowsill and stepped into the quiet apartment.

The temperature inside was almost as cold as out. It was kept from sinking too far only by the walls that held out the wind and the bits of heat that seeped from the surrounding apartments. The thermostat hadn't been adjusted to take into account the sudden cold snap that had come over the area in the last several days. There were still pinpoints of light from the electronics in the living room and flashing on the microwave in the tiny kitchen to the side. The power was still active.

He didn't know if that meant the bill was recently paid up or the owner of the building took care of the utilities. Either way, it made his work easier. He flipped the nearest light switch up. It didn't really matter what light it turned on. He wasn't turning it on to actually use it. The sudden pop of illumination was only for the benefit of anyone who might have seen him going up the back of the building.

It was another way to go unnoticed, even if seen. If a person had watched his progress up the fire escape and through the window, only to go into an apartment and have no light turn on, they might be alarmed. That didn't fit the narrative. It was out of the ordinary. Someone who belonged inside a building in the dark of evening turned on a light.

So he did.

He wasn't worried that someone was going to come out of any of the rooms and see him. He had no concern about someone opening the front door and coming inside. He could take as much time as he needed.

He went from room to room, taking in the frozen seconds that framed the last time anyone had occupied this space. Everything was just as it had been when the woman who lived here stepped out and closed the door for the last time. She probably thought it didn't matter if she put away the pair of boots sagging against the wall right beside the door because she might go out later in the day. The candle sitting on the table in the center of the room had already been burned at least once, but was waiting with a lighter beside it for another round. He didn't see a remote control for the television sitting anywhere out in the open, which meant it was probably shoved down in between the cushions of the couch or under a chair where it always fell. She'd easily find it when she came in wearing her pajamas, the day washed off her face, ready to do her evening form of nothing.

He looked around for the signs of who this woman was. It didn't matter how clean and organized—or even sparse and unwelcoming—an apartment or house was. There were always hints of the person who lived there. It was like water flowing into a container and taking its shape. The space took up the shape of the inhabitant. Little personal items left around. Photographs that caught slivers of what they valued. Decorative touches that brought their taste to the bare walls or empty floor. Even a lingering scent or the temperature it was kept. Every person who lived in a space left part of themselves.

This woman was settled deep into this apartment. It looked like she'd lived here a long time and had sunken into it like another layer of paint on the walls. There were tiny scuffs on the furniture and stains on the carpet. Areas of the walls where wayward hands pressed when she took off her shoes or leaned to get things out of the low cabinets in the dining area were dulled and slightly discolored.

It was easier when it was this way. There were plenty of nooks and corners to put things where they would seem like they had been there all along, even if someone was discovering them for the first time.

He took the items from his pockets and took a few moments to think about how she would use them. He moved through the space like it was his and set them where they felt natural. When he was done, he closed the window and re-engaged the lock, then walked out the front door, ensuring the knob was locked behind him. The deadbolt wasn't engaged, but that didn't make much of a difference. Whoever came next could come to their own conclusions about that.

The ash of nightfall left behind from the sunset cloaked him as he bounced down the front steps of the building. He pulled the collar of his coat close around him against the cool air and a sideways glance from someone coming down the sidewalk. They might have heard his greeting. They might not have. It didn't matter. He was gone before they thought about him again.

⁂

The forecast had promised an unseasonably warm evening with plenty of sunshine through the golden hour. She was glad; it would keep her planned bike ride pleasant enough to push through the extra miles she wanted to achieve. Long stretches of gray skies and a twinged muscle in her thigh had reduced her workouts down to almost nothing over the past several days and the inactivity was starting to get to her.

Cheryl was used to a much more active life before she moved to the big house on the hill in a neighborhood billed as "quiet", but that had proven to feel almost deserted. Not long after she moved in, she set out to find neighbors. Not make friends, necessarily. After all, she wasn't in her patent leather shoes gripping a pack of crayons as she prepared for her first day at a new elementary school. She didn't have her mother running her fingers through her hair at night and reassuring her she would end the week with lots of friends if she just walked into that class determined to be herself.

That advice hadn't really settled too well with her the first time she got it, when her mother really had patted her back and sent her off to an elementary school teeming with unknown faces. Four times.

Be yourself.

Everything will be fine if you just be yourself.

You'll make plenty of friends, just be yourself.

Don't worry about anything. Just be yourself and everything else will fall into place.

What Cheryl never understood was what other option she had. If she waltzed in every day wearing different kinds of clothes, her hair different colors and styles, adopting different dialects and speech patterns, and professing full devotion to a range of hobbies, beliefs, and aversions, did that somehow mean she was a different person every day?

Wasn't it more accurate that she was being herself playing the role of someone with different tastes? Or maybe just a facet of herself she hadn't fully explored? She was still in the same body, using the same brain, the same voice, the same everything. What sort of alchemy was it that made her become an entirely different person because of what she said or wore or did?

What was the difference between Cheryl Bishop and Cheryl Bishop Appearing As…?

And yet, no one was ever able to give her an explanation of the alternative to being herself.

When she'd moved to the new neighborhood, it was her first house where she was just being Cheryl Bishop—and not Cheryl Bishop Appearing As the Dutiful Daughter, or Cheryl Bishop Appearing As the Suburban Housewife, or Cheryl Bishop Appearing As the Widow Whose Sister-in-Law Won't Leave Her Alone. She hadn't set out to be herself and find new friends. She'd just hoped to locate a neighbor or two who she could talk to enough that they might be willing to scrape her off the sidewalk should she take a tumble when out running or biking, or who she could call if something went particularly wrong in her house.

It was a survival effort more than a social move, but having someone she liked hanging out with would be a nice bonus. That would come next. First, knowing some people's names and having them recognize that she existed, and that the old house up on the hill wasn't empty anymore, seemed like a good step.

It was a bit more of a challenge than she had really anticipated. Not that she thought she was going to strap on her shoes for her first run and immediately get showered with welcome, or that she would open her front door and find some smiling woman with a fresh pie and a packet of information about the local businesses in the area. It would be nice, but also just a bit too close to horror movie territory for her comfort. But she also wasn't anticipating being the one that was horror movie fodder for her new neighbors.

The woman who sold her the house had been quick to use all kinds of words like "character" and "history" to describe the house in much the same way that people used "fantastic personality" or "has a real zest for life" to describe a woman when what they really meant was "might have lead paint in the weird mid-century addition with no closets" and "you probably don't want to take this from the dim bar into daylight".

Cheryl had expected that statement to bring along with it all kinds of fun layers of wallpaper or maybe some questionable window treatments. Possibly even a deck or window seat with dubious structural integrity. What she hadn't expected was the way the house seemed to repel people. It was like there was some sort of bubble around it that kept everyone else at bay. Even if people did venture close, their steps got faster as they went by the house, and what might have been friendly glances toward any other house on the block became sharp, fleeting looks through slitted eyes.

It took a couple of weeks before it occurred to her that she'd fulfilled one of the shower thoughts an old friend of hers shared years before.

Every neighborhood has a creepy house full of creepy neighbors that is probably haunted, or at least is where the bodies are buried. If you think that your neighborhood doesn't have one because you've never noticed the creepy neighbors, then you are the creepy neighbors.

Cheryl had officially moved into the neighborhood creepy house and was, therefore, the creepy neighbor.

This definitely didn't top her list of things she wanted to be known for in her life and wasn't the first impression she wanted to make on anyone living on her street. People didn't usually say hello to or try to scoop up and rescue the scary person who chose to move into the potentially haunted house.

She'd been in the house a few months now and so far, her list of people she figured wouldn't watch her go down and leave her there to be reclaimed by the sidewalk was still fairly sparse. There was Bob and Eileen two houses down and Sarah diagonally across the street. Then single mother Maggie on the next block and Rudy who jogged in tracksuits so out of date they'd whipped right back around to being fashionable. Jennifer two streets down with the dog who always barked at her. A Bill somewhere in there.

The long bike ride she had on the docket for that evening might have gone far in helping her map out more of her new neighborhood that was quickly becoming not so new. She didn't want to be six months or a year down the line and still not know the names of the streets or the fastest way to get to her new favorite Thai restaurant. She'd heard a pair of women jogging by talking about the upcoming luminary stroll. She had no idea what that was, but she wanted to find out.

It seemed the universe had different plans for her. That beautiful sunset she'd been promised lasted through her evening commute back but gave way to dense clouds by the time she had her bike shoes on and was walking out to the shed. She'd pedaled her way down three streets by the time the soft mist turned to sprinkles, then another two before it was really rain. By the time she got home, the sun was fully down, she'd met no other neighbors, realized she'd been imagining the name of the street at the end of the block completely wrong, and was soaked to the bone.

Peeling everything off and leaving it in a sopping pile on her mudroom floor, she went into the bathroom and filled the deep clawfoot tub. This tub might just have been worth all the other aggravations of the neighborhood. Who needed a close-knit group of neighborhood friends when she had a bathtub with feet long enough to stretch out and deep enough to sink down to chin level?

The ride hadn't been as long or intense as she had wanted it to be, but she'd still done it. The effort had pushed the injured muscle in her leg a little further than she'd meant it to, so she figured she deserved a hot soak to the soothing sound of the rain. At least then the sudden downpour hadn't completely betrayed her.

She drifted away, surrounded by the scent of her favorite candle and lush bubbles. The combination had her dangerously close to falling asleep in the water when a crash overhead snapped her back awake. It seemed the warm day and the sudden cool snap that rolled in with the later evening weren't getting along. Her window lit up with a flash of lightning and Cheryl scrambled to get out of the tub.

Her mother might not have gained a lot of credence with her friend-making recommendations, but she was spot-on with her warning never to take a bath or shower in a storm. Science backed her up on that one. Cheryl's understanding of whether being submerged in a couple of feet of water in a clawfoot tub was better or worse than a conventional tub was a bit shaky, but what she did know was that she didn't want to be a cautionary tale for those who didn't want to show respect to the unhinged electricity tearing the sky into pieces overhead.

She dried off and risked a fast dip of her hand back into the water to tug on the chain that released the drain plug, so the water, bubbles, and relaxation disappeared.

Cheryl put on the pants and threadbare shirt she picked out for sleep and covered them with a robe as she walked through the house toward the kitchen. Her mama had never given her any warnings about eating during a storm, so she decided now was the time for dinner.

What time was it, anyway? She looked around for her phone, before remembering she'd left it behind before her ride, as she always did. She went to the nightstand and picked it up—and was dismayed to find that it was dead. With a sigh, she placed it on the charger and looked up at the wall clock. It was eleven forty PM.

The bowl she put her salads in was technically a mixing bowl, but she didn't care. It was easier to toss the vegetables around with the dressing and seasoning, and she could cover it with plastic wrap and shove it right into the refrigerator like that to save for the next day if she got full. The cabinets and appliances weren't judging her, and considering they were the only ones around to watch her convert an entire container of spring mix and several other whole vegetables chopped to little pieces into what was ostensibly a meal for one person, she didn't feel the compulsion to change her ways.

She finished tossing the salad and set it on the table, then went to the refrigerator in search of some protein to add to it. A container of marinated chicken tossed around in a pan on the stove finished it up and she settled in to listen to the rain and eat. She got several bites in before the first wave of dizziness hit her. It had been a long day at work; she considered for a moment whether to crack open the new bottle of red wine she'd picked up a few days before. She deserved it, she reasoned: her evening plans had sputtered into dust and now that the clock was rapidly approaching midnight, she may as well give herself a treat.

She savored the wine, humming in delight as it slid down her throat. She savored the slow, steady sound of the clock ticking, blending with the pummeling of rain outside. *Tick, tick, tick.*

She got several bites in before the first wave of dizziness hit her.

It was that strange swaying feeling of motion sickness, but without going anywhere. She set down her fork and took a breath. It might have been too long between meals, especially with her ride. Maybe she hadn't had enough water. She tried a few more bites before nausea set in. The lights started flickering overhead and before Cheryl could push away from the table, they went out completely.

The house fell utterly silent. Without the familiar hum of the refrigerator or the barely audible presence of the lights, she finally understood why this house was so creepy. All she could hear was the steady, rhythmic marching of each second passing on the wall clock. *Tick, tick, tick.*

She stood up on shaky legs, ready to head back to the bedroom to grab her phone, but her balance slipped from under her and the wine glass tipped over with a tinkling crash, spilling all over the table and dripping onto the floor. She cursed under her breath and promised herself to pick it up when she could see.

She gripped the edge of the table to help her navigate the dark room as she tried to remember where she last saw a flashlight or an emergency candle. Her brain didn't seem to want to connect. It was a simple question. Where was the flashlight? But she couldn't figure it out. She didn't know if it was the darkness around her, the increasing volume of the thunder that was shaking the floor beneath her feet, or the continuing waves of sickness that had her hoping she could hold onto her salad, but she felt disoriented and confused.

Tick, tick, tick.

Her hands shook as she pulled open a drawer and dug through it. There wasn't anything inside that would help her and she dug through two more before leaving the kitchen. Her hand slid down the wall in the hallway as she used it to hold her up. Her mind drifted back to the first time she'd toured the house with the woman who told her about its character and history.

The walls were a freshly painted, nice eggshell.

White?

Eggshell.

What was the difference? And what the hell was ecru?

Tick, tick, tick.

Cheryl leaned back against the wall and closed her eyes, fighting the tossing of her stomach and the jumbling of her mind. She couldn't make her thoughts fall into place enough to remember anything. Finally, she made it to the bathroom. Dropping to her knees on the tile, she leaned to press her cheek against the cool side of the tub. The room still held a bit of the heat and dampness from the bath, the air tinged just slightly with the scent of her bubbles and the last wisps of the candle she'd been burning on the counter.

She reached up for it and her fingertips pushed the candle into the basin of the sink. Waiting to make sure her stomach was going to allow her the movement without protesting, she dragged herself along the floor until she could pull up on the counter and pull the candle out. She managed to find the lighter and stared at it in her trembling hand. It was so dark in the room she could only just make out the very edges of her palm and the small rectangle in it.

Tick, tick, tick.

A brilliant purple flash of light outside brightened the room and made her scream. The candle pressed into the center of her chest felt hard against her ribs and did little to calm the frantic beating of her heart. It couldn't find its rhythm. Like it was torn between what it should be doing and the uneasiness of the rest of her body.

She pulled the candle away and tried to light it, but her fingers couldn't work the lighter. Finally, a small flame appeared, and she touched it to the wick. She sat there on the floor, staring at the lit candle, trying to connect the glow of light to what was happening around her.

Tick, tick, tick.

The disorientation was only getting worse as she finally made her way into her bedroom. She was too dizzy to walk straight down the hallway and had to lean with her back against the wall to slide her way there. She didn't understand what was happening. This wasn't from going too long between meals or being dehydrated. Something else was affecting her.

Tick.

She finally grabbed at her phone on the bedside table and moved to turn it on, but it didn't respond. Panic flooded her now as she tried again to turn on her phone. She pulled it close to her with shaky hands—and then discovered that the cord hadn't been plugged into the wall this entire time. She couldn't call for help.

Tick.

She just barely sat on the bed before stumbling over and hurling into her small trashcan. She briefly considered going back to the bathroom, but she was shaking too hard. Her head spun with the dizzy, confused feeling. All she wanted was to lie down. As her body curled up on the comforter, she stared at the candle flickering inches away.

Tick.

She blew it out, then instantly wished she hadn't. The lighter was in the bathroom. The storm still raged outside. Her phone was still out of power. She got sick again, this time feeling like it took every bit of energy she had left inside her. The last thing she heard before her eyes closed was the soft chime of the wall clock announcing the time.

Midnight.

CHAPTER ONE

"You said you loved her."

"I did, Emma. I still do."

"You could never do something like that to someone you love."

"Emma, you have to understand…"

"No. That's the thing. I don't have to understand. I don't have to and I'm never going to. You will never be able to make me think the way that you do or see things the same way that you do. You will never be able to make me understand how you could possibly do the things that you've done and still stand there and say that you feel love and compassion like a real human being."

"Then why are you asking me these questions? Why do you even want to know?"

Those are questions I've asked myself more times than I can even count over the last almost eleven months. I've actually asked myself far longer than that, it's just that this last year has been the only time I've had the real opportunity to do anything about the constant barrage of questions bouncing around in my head.

"Because I have to," I finally say.

On the other end of the line, Jonah is quiet. That's the state when I find him the most unnerving. I never want to say I find him frightening because I've spent too much of my life giving him that power. I refuse to let him control me any longer. He doesn't deserve my fear. But it's useless to pretend he's something that he isn't. A man doesn't cause the level of destruction and death he has without carrying a heaviness over him.

Even if he can't wrap his head around the reality of it.

I'm on my way to Harlan. The first couple of hours of the trip, I drove in silence. My thoughts over the last few weeks have been plenty to keep me occupied no matter what I'm doing. Including wishing I was asleep. The darkest depths of night aren't unfamiliar to me; that dip in existence right before the sun starts to come up when everything seems to have stopped and there might be no end seems to be the space I've been trapped in. I've spent plenty of those hours sitting up staring into the distance, digging through case files until my fingertips are raw and the words have broken down to just a scattering of letters across the paper, or watching the neighborhood sleep through my living room window.

I thought those days were over. The last time I went through a stretch of not being able to sleep, it pushed me right to the brink. There were days when I didn't know if I was actually experiencing what I thought I was or if it was all the desperate reactions of my sleep-deprived mind. But in a lot of ways, that was preferable to what was waiting on the other side of falling asleep.

When I did manage to slip away for a short time, it was into my nightmares. They haven't found me yet this time, but I can't imagine they are going to take long if I don't start sleeping better soon.

I probably would have driven the entire way with only my thoughts to keep me occupied if my phone hadn't rung. It was sitting in the plastic cradle attached to the dashboard, giving me directions I didn't actually need. I've made this trip what feels like hundreds of times over the last few years. It happened to ring just as I was going through one of the very few places of congested traffic in the route between Sherwood and Harlan, so I didn't get the chance to check the screen and see who was calling.

Most of the time I would just ignore the call and check it when I got a second after getting through the mess. But Sam is still out of town helping his Aunt Rose look for his missing cousin. Marie has not been heard from in a couple of weeks now and what started as mere curiosity has become worry, and is rapidly turning to fear.

Rose didn't think the local police up in Michigan were doing enough to try to find out what happened to Marie and where she might be, so she called Sam. As a third-generation Sheriff of Sherwood, he has both the family connection and the understanding of law enforcement she wants to provide her comfort and reassurance in this situation—and as my husband, he has experience with a wide range of reasons for people to go missing.

That means he's a great addition to the search for Marie, but it also means he's been away for a while, and I miss him so much. He wanted me to go with him, but I've been too deeply buried in cases to leave, which is why I was eager to answer thinking it might be Sam. Instead, a chill slithered down my spine when the voice on the other side of the line was Jonah.

He's caused more pain and difficulty in my life than anyone else ever has, including throwing me headlong into the cases that kept me from going with Sam and still have me tangled up. The man actually responsible for a murder that Jonah was accused of committing is dead, but that hasn't ended the questions. In a lot of ways, it has only left more.

Which is nothing new when it comes to Jonah. He isn't just a terrorist, serial killer, and violent, sociopathic cult leader. He isn't just an escaped convict with untold numbers of devotees ready and willing to lay down their lives to protect him. He isn't just a brilliant, resourceful man with delusions of grandeur and aspirations of dominion over a broken human race.

He's my uncle. My father's identical twin brother. The reason my mother is dead.

I wish I never have to think about him, but I don't have a choice. He's there. A part of my bloodline. Inescapable. Cutting Jonah out of my existence would be no different than shearing a branch off a tree. It is never really gone. Parts of it will always remain. No matter how deep you cut or far you think you've gone at getting rid of it, it's impossible to fully separate what was created and grew together.

And because of that, there were questions I would always have if I don't ask them. Things I need to know even if I will never be able to understand.

"What is it that you want to know? What do you want me to tell you?" Jonah asks.

"The truth. That's what I've always asked you to give me, and it seems you have a really hard time giving it to me," I say.

"I do give you the truth, Emma. I tell you the truth that I have to tell you. That doesn't mean it's always going to be what you want to hear or what you think I should be telling you. It means it's the truth I have to give you. I can promise you that, but nothing else."

I don't like to compromise with him. I don't like giving him space or offering him grace. But I know I have to. It's the only way I can get what I need from him, whether it's the answers to my questions and the details about my past that only he holds, or the bits and pieces I need to put together to find him and get him back behind bars where he belongs.

He knows I'm chasing him. He knows every time he calls me that I filter every bit of information I can glean out of the conversation through my desire to find him. It makes him measure out what he says and dose out details so I'm always catching up.

"I want to know how you can say that you loved my mother. Even now, after everyone knows everything."

"Why would that change anything?"

"At one time, you might have been able to get some sympathy. Before all this came to light. But now…" I take a second to calm the anger rushing up inside me. Sometimes I still struggle with the reality of all the horror that this man caused. It's especially hard to think about what he did to my mother. "Why do you still disrespect her by saying you loved her?"

"I did love her. I do love her. I've never stopped. I loved her the minute I met her. That's never going to change. I would never do anything to disrespect her."

"You had her killed!"

"I did *not* have her killed!"

The words explode out of Jonah with a force and anger that surprises me. He's usually almost eerily calm and controlled. It's not like him to show that much emotion.

"She is dead because of you," I growl, not willing to let up at all. "You sent those men to our house."

"They weren't there for Mariya," Jonah protests, his voice low, sounding like the cold fog rolling over swamp water.

It sends a chill rolling through me, but it's not fear or discomfort. It's anger. Because I know exactly why they were there. I know why he sent them and what they were supposed to do. I know when they broke into the Florida house where we lived, a house I forgot after that night, and opened fire on the shadow they saw coming toward them, they thought they were filling my father with lead.

Instead, they were leaving my mother in a pool of blood.

"Oh, that makes it so much better. You *meant* to kill my father. You wanted your own brother dead."

"To protect her. To protect you," he insists.

"There was nothing to protect us from," I snap. "He never hurt us. He was everything to her. She loved him."

I hear him take in a long breath. He's clearly trying to get himself under control. He doesn't want to hear that. It's enough to make me want to say it over and over.

"She loved me," he says.

"No. No, Jonah. She never loved you. She loved my father. She always loved him. There was never a second guess in her mind. You were obsessed with her. Enough to rape her and then try to claim me as yours."

"Don't say that," he says. "Never say that. I wouldn't hurt her."

"You killed her."

I pull off the side of the road, the conversation making me shake and blurring my vision. Turning off the car, I lean my head back and close my eyes. I need to get myself together to get through the rest of this drive.

"I didn't kill her. She wasn't supposed to be there. She wasn't supposed to be home."

"If you really loved her, you would have wanted her to be happy. That would have been the most important thing to you."

"You don't really believe that, do you, Emma?"

CHAPTER TWO

"How did you turn into this?" I ask after the sting of his last question leaves my skin. "How did you become what you are?"

"I am what I am. There was no becoming."

"I can't accept that," I reply.

"I wish there was something I could tell you that would help you understand," he says.

"Tell me what happened. Tell me how it happened. Look me in the eyes and tell me what I deserve to know."

"You know I can't do that. Not now."

My phone clicks and I see that a call from Dean is coming in on the other line.

"I have to go," I say. "Dean is calling. He's waiting for me."

"Dean?" Jonah asks, his voice lifting slightly. "How is he?"

"I'm not talking to you about Dean."

"I want to talk to him," he says.

"You did talk to him. The day he came to see you in the prison. He told you he wasn't ever going to think of you again, and that's what he meant. He never wanted to think about you again. Don't you get that?" I snap. "He doesn't want to have anything to do with you."

"No," Jonah says. "I'm his father. I have the right—"

"Listen to me, Jonah. There is one thing that Dean and I have in common that connected us even before we knew we were cousins. You are the reason neither one of us has a mother. The only reason he was born at all was because you were so obsessed with my mother you had to live out your sick fantasies with a woman who looked and sounded like her, and who you knew had a connection with her," I say.

"I didn't know he was my son. I thought she'd had him with someone else."

"And you think that makes a difference?" I scoff bitterly. "Somehow you think that because you didn't know that using her to deal with being fixated on your brother's wife—a woman who wanted nothing to do with you and never would—had resulted in a child, that it was alright that you murdered her? Because that's the one major separation right there.

"You can say as many times as you want that it wasn't your fault my mother died because you didn't send those men for her, but you absolutely intended for Dean's mother to die. You wanted to get rid of her. She wasn't amusing to you anymore, so you treated her like a piece of trash you had the right to just toss away. And you left a boy with no one. To fend for himself and suffer whatever the world was going to throw at him. No one will ever know what he could have been, what he might have accomplished or achieved.

"You took that. You stole that from him and from the rest of the world. When you killed his mother, you killed the man Dean was going to grow up to be. It is nothing short of a miracle he was able to overcome the shit you fed him to and become the man he is, and even that man is scarred. He suffers and he struggles, and there will never be a second of his life that he isn't aware that it's because of you. There was an entire life he should have lived but he never got to, because you decided what you wanted was more important.

"But that doesn't mean you are entitled to even a second of his conscious, purposeful thought. You don't deserve for him to wonder about you or want to know anything about you."

"And yet, you do," Jonah replies. "You want to know me."

"I want to know what caused you," I clarify. "Dean does not want to think about you. But he has no choice. You've managed to find yet another way to force yourself into his existence. He doesn't have the option not to have you go through his mind every day. He's still trying to recover from being abducted and forced to fight for his life in a gladiator arena."

"I didn't do that to him. I had no idea that would happen to him," Jonah insists.

"You caused it," I fire back. "Salvador Marini punished Serena for her allegiance to you, and he went after Dean because of his connection to you. Dean suffered and continues to suffer even though he has and wants absolutely no relationship with you."

"The man responsible is dead now," Jonah says.

"So there was no justice. He wasn't forced to face all the people he'd hurt and the families of the ones he murdered. He was never held accountable for everything he caused. We won't get the answers we need. He'll never have to deal with even a day of punishment in their names."

"He was destined for far worse punishment," Jonah huffs.

"No," I snap. "Don't. Don't even try to invoke God in this."

I know I'm treading deep. I'm pushing him and it might backfire on me. My original intention when he started contacting me was to do everything I could to draw information out of him so I could both solve the cases he pushed me into and find him. It's a delicate, careful balance. I despise this man for everything he's done and everything I know he wouldn't hesitate for a second to do, but I have to be willing to engage with him and attempt to earn his trust so I can get from him what I need.

But I can't do it. Not today. Not while I'm on my way to see Dean and try to help him through yet another painful struggle as he fights to keep hold of his memories and not slip into the darkness that sometimes takes him.

"You've been willing to talk to me. You've let me call you. You've reached out to me yourself. Why can't he?"

"Don't mistake this for bonding, Jonah. I'm not doing this for you. This isn't a family reunion. I've been willing to speak to you because there are people who are dead and others who are missing. They need a voice and I am here to make sure that you are never, ever that voice for them. Every single one of them, regardless of who they were, deserve better than that," I say.

"Then why don't I?" he asks.

"Xavier once told me that even the most open field in the world has a fence somewhere. You are my barbed wire."

I end the call and pull away from the side of the road and continue on my way toward the house where Xavier and Dean live.

By the time I pull into the driveway, the afternoon is getting deep, taking on that dark blue edge that seems closer in the later months of the year. I pull into the driveway and finally cut the engine, letting out a breath it feels like I've been holding ever since leaving the side of the road. The door opens and Xavier's head pops out. He stares at my car for a few seconds, then disappears back inside.

His reaction doesn't surprise me. He isn't a puppy. I don't expect him to come bounding out to the car to greet me. In the time I've known him, I've learned to try to interpret his actions not from my own perspective or the one I assume other people in my life have, but from what little of Xavier's perspective I understand. If I had to guess, that reaction was that he was checking to see if the sound of the car was me arriving, he looked out and confirmed it was, and then he went back inside because there wasn't anything else he needed to do.

Seconds later, the door opens again. This time it's Dean. He comes down the front steps with a slight hobble and meets me at the side of the car.

"What can I carry for you?" he asks.

I shake my head. "Nothing. I'm fine. You go on inside. It's cold out here. Go sit down."

"I'm tired of sitting down," he gripes. "Xavier says that to me all day. Even when I'm already sitting down."

"He knows you're thinking about standing up," I shrug, going around to the trunk of my car and opening it so I can haul out my two overstuffed duffels.

"You know," Dean says, walking alongside me as we head up the sidewalk, "I really wouldn't put that past him."

"How are you feeling?" I ask.

"Same as I was when you asked me yesterday," he says. "And this morning."

There's a gloss of bitterness over the teasing. I know he's frustrated and doesn't want to take it out on me. But I would understand even if he did. What he went through is unimaginable—and even worse is not knowing all of what happened or how. He doesn't want to give in to the pain, but some of his injuries will take a lot of time to heal. Dean is no stranger to that. His career in the special forces was cut short because of an injury.

I don't worry about his body nearly as much as I worry about his mind. A memory lapse cost him the time between when he stepped out of his house and when he was found discarded by the side of the road, bruised and bloody. It was only after my good friend Eric was taken in the same manner that we realized he'd apparently escaped a gladiator fight put on to entertain the killer who called himself the Emperor.

Dean doesn't know when he was taken or by who. How he was transported or what happened while he was there.

The thought of what he might have left there haunts him.

CHAPTER THREE

"Is everything alright?" Dean asks as I set down my bags and drop down into one of the big chairs in the living room. "I called and you didn't answer. We thought you were going to get here earlier."

"I know. I thought I was going to, too. But then I got a fairly unwelcome phone call on the way," I say.

"From who?"

"Whom," Xavier chimes in. "From whom?"

I meet Dean's eyes and the way his face darkens tells me he knows exactly who called me. "What did he want?"

"To know about the investigation into his escape," I sigh. "He wants me to tell him what the prison knows and if anyone has talked."

"Did you tell him?" Xavier asks.

"Of course, not," I say. "I mean, there really isn't anything to tell him."

"That is something you could tell him. But then telling him that would be having something to tell him, so it would be a fundamental logical fallacy. I suppose you could tell him there is nothing of note to tell him, but I find that problematic as well, because you are, in essence, making note of the lack of noteworthy discovery from the investigation. From that perspective, it's probably just safer to say you have nothing to tell him."

"Thank you, Xavier," I say. He nods and goes back to the puzzle he's working on. It's most of the way finished, which means he probably started it when I turned onto the street. I look back at Dean. "I didn't tell him that no one has been able to figure out how he escaped. It's something I'm holding for leverage. Unfortunately, I think he's doing the same thing."

"What kind of leverage would it give him?" he asks. "He's already out. He already managed to get past not only all of the technology and mechanical systems put into place to control inmate movement throughout the facility, but also all the guards and officers who were supposed to be watching him. It's a massive embarrassment to everyone working in that facility and kind of to the entire law enforcement community. It wouldn't do a whole lot of good for him to rub it in their faces by explaining how he did it."

"No, but it might ensure they can stop it from happening again," I point out. "Until they can figure out the sequence of events and the specific failures that had to happen for him to escape, they aren't going to be able to say with total confidence that they are a secure facility. And that other inmates aren't going to do the same thing."

"No other inmates are going to do the same thing," Dean counters. "No one would be able to figure it out."

"I could," Xavier says.

"The thing is, as much as everyone wants to believe that there were a ton of inside people helping him and he was able to get out because he was let out, I really don't think that's the case," I say.

"Neither do I," Xavier says. "He got himself out."

"But how?" Dean asks. "That is one of the most intensely guarded, advanced security facilities in the country. The only thing it doesn't do is keep the prisoners inside their cells twenty-four hours a day. How could he possibly find a way to get out that doesn't involve other people?"

"I didn't say it definitely didn't involve other people," I say. "I just said it didn't necessarily involve working with the guards or bribing them somehow. Jonah had a lot of time in there to figure out how he was going to get past all those measures to get out when he wanted to. He admitted he and Serena had several different plans and were still trying to sort through them, but there are notes and descriptions in her code that I'm sure will eventually explain exactly how he did it."

"I could do it," Xavier repeats.

"Of course you could," Dean says. "You could do it a lot faster and more easily than Jonah. No prison could hold you."

I cringe as he says it and give my cousin a pained look. "Dean."

There's a brief second when it seems he doesn't even realize what he said, then that hint of confusion disappears and is replaced by shock.

"Xavier, I'm so sorry," he says. "I didn't even think..."

Xavier shakes his head. "It's alright."

"No," Dean says. "No, it's not. I got myself so worked up I didn't even think about what I was saying."

"Dean, it's alright," Xavier says. "You're right."

"What do you mean?"

"I could have done it a lot faster and more easily than Jonah. Now, that's just my assumption based on the available evidence. But, yes, I could have. And, no, no prison could hold me."

"But Xavier," I say gently. I don't want to shake something loose in him and cause problems, but there's an obvious issue in what he's saying and I'm waiting for it to come to his mind. When it doesn't, I lean a little closer, hoping to pull his attention away from the puzzle. "You spent eight years in prison."

He makes a noncommittal face and gives half a shrug. "Jail, prison, the alternative detention center. If you want to combine all of them into one general punitive concept, then, yes, about eight years."

I'm waiting for him to break it down for me by months, weeks, days, and even hours, since I have no doubt in my mind he has that information right at the tip of his tongue. But he doesn't give it to me. I look at Dean, who shakes his head slightly like he's telling me I'm the one who got myself into this whole conversation and now it's my turn to try to fix it.

I continue to watch Xavier, waiting for his thoughts to meander their way down whatever path they are currently following so he can circle back around to where Dean and I are. But he doesn't seem to see anything problematic about his assertions.

"Xavier, you were in for that long," I say, shifting the emphasis on the words to help him along.

He looks up at me and blinks. "Oh, I know. It was my sentence. But if I'd wanted to leave, I could have. That was one of my favorite games I played when I ran out of books to read from the visiting bookmobile cart. I called it 'Hypothetical Prison Break: How I Would Take Advantage of Evident Weaknesses and Shortcomings in the Detention System to Escape and Take On a New Identity and Life Elsewhere.'"

I point at him as I look at Dean. "That is how you market a fun family game night experience."

"You just came up with ways that you were going to break out of prison?" Dean raises an eyebrow.

"Well, whatever facility I happened to be in at the time. Or van. That was more challenging since I also had to hypothetically have a driver's license," Xavier explains.

"You were planning ways to escape from prison," I point out. "I think you could give yourself a bit of wiggle room when it came to the legality of driving a prison van."

"Also, it probably should have been more pressing that you don't actually know how to drive," Dean adds.

"Technicality," Xavier says dismissively.

"Kind of a big one," Dean says.

"Wait, can we get back to you planning ways to break out of prison?" I ask.

"Not planning," Xavier corrects me. "Pondering. For fun."

"Yes. Fun," I nod. "But here's the thing. You didn't do anything wrong. You were innocent and knew you were. So why did you stay? Far be it from me to encourage people to go against the justice system, but you gave up eight years of your life for something you didn't do. If you figured out all these ways to get out, why didn't you? You could have gone off and started a new life. No one would have been hurt."

"I'm not a criminal, Emma," he says.

"I know you're not," I say. "That's the point. You were convicted of a crime you didn't commit. Something you didn't have anything to do with at all. You have no criminal history at all. No arrests. No tickets."

"That's a silver lining to not driving," he smiles. "No possibility of traffic infractions when you aren't part of traffic."

"Very true," I acknowledge. "But you were a part of a prison population. And you ended up in solitary confinement for a good part of it, again for something you didn't do."

I can't believe I'm actually standing here arguing with a man for not escaping from prison. This is not a position I ever thought I'd find myself in. But that's something that's come with age and gathering the people I've surrounded myself with over the last several years. I never stop learning. Or, in some very specific cases, getting thrown headlong into reality like getting smashed into a brick wall.

This is closer to one of those situations.

"I'm not a criminal," Xavier repeats. "I was put in prison for something I didn't do. That doesn't mean I let them turn me into what they wanted me to be."

"A person who is afraid of dogs will be afraid of all of them even if they aren't dangerous," Dean says, nodding in that way I'm sure I do when I try to channel Xavier in what I think or say. "Putting it in a cage only makes it worse."

Xavier stares at him for an almost uncomfortably long second, then looks back at me.

"A person whose first marshmallow was stale will not like marshmallows because they think they are all stale. If they buy a bag of marshmallows, tear it open, and leave it like that for a while, they'll come back to stale marshmallows and it will be exactly what they thought. It's not the marshmallow's fault. It was wonderful and squishy at first. That person made it stale and fulfilled their own prejudice.

"But that doesn't change what it has become. It is still a stale marshmallow. You can toast it. You can put it in cereal. But you can never go back. It might be understandable, but it's not acceptable. And it's not inevitable. Just because someone thinks something of you doesn't mean you let them change you. Sometimes you can't stop it. A dog put in a cage is at the mercy of its instincts. A marshmallow can't climb back into the bag, it has no opposable thumbs.

"But if there is a change you can prevent and you don't, it is your fault, and you are no better than if it was true. Possibly worse. I did nothing wrong. I wasn't a criminal when they arrested me or when they convicted me or when they put me in prison. I wasn't going to turn myself into one afterward. I knew one day I wouldn't be there anymore."

"Because someone would exonerate you," I say, thinking of Lakyn Monroe and the work she was doing to try to find the truth about Xavier.

"Or I'd die there."

"Oh."

"But either way, I would leave. And I'd leave the same way I went in. Not a criminal."

"And no moving violations," I add.

Dean stands up and starts out of the room.

"Dean…" Xavier says.

"I'm already on it."

CHAPTER FOUR

The smell of the marshmallows roasting in the fireplace makes me miss my grandmother and feel nostalgic for Christmas. It's one of those memories I didn't even know I had until I breathed in the sticky sweet scent with its fine edge of carbon and got a strong, visceral memory of sitting in the living room with my family, the Christmas tree visible out of the corner of my eye, as I held a marshmallow pierced on the end of a straightened-out wire coat hanger into the center of orange flames.

I don't know what house that was, or even how old I was in the memory. But it fills me with a sudden rush of holiday spirit and longing that's almost sad.

"Would now be a bad time to ask if there have been any new developments on your case?" I ask.

"I can't really think of a particularly good time," Dean replies. "And it's not really a case."

"Of course it is," I say. "You were attacked."

"By someone doing it at the bidding of a man who's dead now," he points out. "It's not like anything can be done about it."

He doesn't want to be the focus. He doesn't want the attention, and I know that. Dean doesn't like being at the center of anything, even when he wants to know the truth. He is angry about what happened and wants answers to all his questions, but he doesn't want to be a victim. He'd rather be seen as evidence.

"That doesn't mean we shouldn't find out what happened," I say. "Salvador might be gone, but someone was helping him. You know that as well as I do. This is a man who called himself the Emperor. I would venture to say there were probably a couple of people helping him at any given time. He just had his favorites."

It's hard to imagine that he didn't have more than one person helping him. Many serial killers have a fairly small turf, staying close to their own neighborhood or other comfort zones. Some spread out more, traveling or moving around as they kill. The Emperor was different. He killed in many different places, but they weren't random. It was a precise calculation.

This wasn't a man who saw people and compulsively decided to kill them. He was far too arrogant for that. This wasn't an impulse. It wasn't something he could have said was uncontrollable. I've been in the FBI long enough to know the compulsion to kill isn't as simple as many people want it to be. It's much easier to think there is a clear line between those who are capable of killing and those who aren't.

People want to think a human being comes into this world evil or good, able to kill or not. They want someone who kills to be vicious and cruel. That's something I hear all the time when interviewing witnesses in various cases: "he wasn't a killer", people insist. As if the goodness and kindness someone shows the world reflects even to their innermost, deepest truths. It's horrible to wrap your head around someone killing a person you love simply to express the brutality and contempt for human life within them. It's unimaginable to try to cope with death that comes at the hands of someone who chose randomly, who can't claim any reason behind it because they were fueled by the voices in their head or by some pathology that put them, in the eyes of many, in the position of victimhood.

But that was not the Emperor. Every death was carefully and meticulously planned. He had no need to rush or to hide. In fact, he went out of his way to make sure everything was exactly to his liking. These deaths, and the horrors that happened to his female victims before they actually got to the mercy of death, were for nothing more than his entertainment.

He didn't kill to make a statement. He wasn't sending a message or trying to prove something. He wasn't punishing anyone in particular. He wasn't even delusional enough to believe the murders he committed would give him power or righteous purpose to the world.

This was pure selfish indulgence. He used the women to fulfill his desires and the men for sport. It was to amuse himself and nothing more.

The only one who deviated from that is Serena. The death that brought the case to my doorstep. Her murder went unexplained for many long months before I joined the investigation in Breyer. And the only reason they brought me in was that they suspected Jonah of killing her. He swore he didn't do it and asked me to be the one to dig into the case and prove he wasn't the one who left the beautiful young woman in the snow to die.

It would be an unbelievable understatement to say having to defend Jonah and try to clear his name was one of the most difficult moments of my career. After everything I went through to get him in prison, the thought of not only having to deal with him escaping but also fighting to clear his name made me sick.

But I couldn't just turn my back. It wasn't about him. I don't care what anyone thinks of him. What I do care about is making sure the stories of all the victims are told correctly. Just having someone blamed isn't good enough. A scapegoat doesn't rectify the stain of murder. Even more than that, the path of proving Jonah didn't kill Serena, whose identity wasn't even known until after I joined the investigation, also led to the discovery of the serial killer who had gone unnoticed for many years.

I'm not necessarily ready to go so far as to say Jonah did a good deed, but it was a lesson in humanity and in what my priorities and morals really are.

Even when it's uncomfortable.

"Do you think the person helping him at the end was around during the other murders?" Dean asks. "Or did they get picked up to replace Serena?"

I shake my head. "I don't know. She helped him select them and bring them to him. I doubt she was actually there for the murders themselves, but she was an intrinsic part of the process. There haven't been any signs of who the other person is or if they were involved in anything before she died."

"Simon and Wheeler haven't been able to find anything, either," he says. "The unspoken opinion right now is that there isn't really anywhere else to go with the investigation right now. With Marini dead, the chances of getting any new information are really slim until we're able to find where some of the other victims were killed or identify other victims that we can link to him."

"We just have to keep looking," I say. "It wouldn't be the first time murders were identified as being linked to a serial killer well after that killer died."

I stare into the fire and watch the edges of my marshmallow bubble and singe.

"What is it, Emma?" Xavier asks.

I shake my head slightly. "Just thinking about Salvador Marini's death. There was something about it that's just not sitting right with me. I don't know how to explain it, it's just something that wasn't right."

"They say he had a heart attack," Dean says. "He was probably shocked that he got caught and under a tremendous amount of stress and anxiety after confessing. It just put too much strain on him. We don't know what kind of lifestyle he was living before all this. I don't think it's too big of a leap of the imagination to think a dude who fancied himself a Roman Emperor and killed people for entertainment might have been decadent in other areas of his life. Food, drink, drugs. All of that could have made him more vulnerable."

"That's true," I acknowledge, "but I just… something was off. He was in fantastic shape, and I know people who look like they are in amazing shape die from heart attacks all the time, but the autopsy didn't find any indications of long-term damage, heart disease, or anything else that would make having a heart attack make sense."

"But there also wasn't anything that would indicate it was anything but a heart attack," Dean points out.

I pull the marshmallow out of the fire and blow out the flames before gingerly pulling some of it away. It burns and I quickly shove my thumb in my mouth to suck off the sticky molten sugar.

"I know," I say. I let out a sigh. "I know."

There are so many questions hanging over us. Even if I push aside the suspicious thoughts about his death, there's still so much we don't understand. The Emperor's long string of murders happened in so many places and with so many methods, and Dean was only the latest in a long string of men who found themselves with a lapse in memory and a bruised body after their ordeals in the gladiator pit. I know there are very likely survivors we don't know about. I assumed the fights didn't end with both of the contestants dying. If that were the case, there would have been more instances of two or more bodies being found around the same time.

Instead, most of the fights were probably similar to the one Eric nearly died in, where one of the competitors had been involved in several fights already and kept captive in between. We need to find those survivors. We need to talk to them and find out what they can tell us about their experiences.

The man Eric fought against is alive, but in even worse condition than he is. Both are still in the hospital. We haven't been able to get much information out of him and I doubt there will be much we'll learn any time soon, if at all. I know Dean's blackouts have contributed to him not remembering what happened the day he was taken, but I don't think it's the only thing. Something else happened. Something else made it so the other men brought for the amusement of the Emperor were under control and did as they were commanded.

The possibility the men were drugged in some way isn't a stab in the dark. Serena's cause of death was technically exposure, but the reason she was out in that field, dressed in a way that wasn't at all appropriate for the season, was the LSD he dosed her with, during what was meant to be the encounter she broke ties with him.

I'm still hopeful what we found in the train station locker and in the office at the house where she was living will give up more information about Serena, her time in Leviathan, and what really happened between her and Salvador Marini. But except for a couple of the recordings, everything was done in code. Unless we can break the code or get someone who understands it to translate for us, we won't know everything she left behind.

And considering the only person I know for sure has the best chances of understanding the code is Jonah, I have little hope. He won't tell me where he is or how he got out of prison. He says he's not ready to go back to prison, that there are still things he needs to do, so he has to keep himself ahead and never let any of us get too close.

For now, as much as I want to push him about it, I force myself to hold back. I got close to completely losing control on the phone with him earlier, but I don't think I went far enough to totally break ties with him. I have to keep the balance. I need him to stay willing to talk to me. Which means I can't rely on him to answer these questions for me. I have to figure them out for myself.

CHAPTER FIVE

"Have you found out anything else about Miley Stanford?" Dean asks.

"No. Jonah keeps skimming around it. He knows more than he's telling me. He specifically admitted that he chose for Serena to take over Miley's life. That wasn't a fluke. And it doesn't seem like something that just sprung up out of nowhere. But I don't know if he actually knows everything that happened to her."

"You don't?"

I shake my head.

"I can't believe these words are about to come out of my mouth about Jonah for the second time in just a few months, but I believe him. He told me there were still things I needed to figure out. That there were still questions and that this situation wasn't over. Then he asked where

Miley is. To me, that means he doesn't know exactly where she is or what happened to her.

"I think he has an idea. He has some concept of what might have led to her disappearance. But I really don't think he knows exactly what happened to her. I think that's part of why he made sure Serena was there in her house. And maybe why Serena was involved with Salvador. She was manipulating him. Taking advantage of him for the benefit of Leviathan. But also gathering information to blackmail him."

"That's not Leviathan's usual style. There was something more to that. Not that Leviathan doesn't manipulate or resort to blackmail to get what they want out of people, but it's usually something much bigger than this. Salvador was wealthy, I'll give him that. And he did have some influence. But it wasn't like he was an extremely powerful political force or ran several companies. As far as we've been able to tell so far, he didn't have anything to do with drug or weapons trades, which is much more of Leviathan's bread and butter."

As the evening grows deeper and the bag of marshmallows begins to wane, we let the conversation drift away from the cases that have been dominating my attention and over to less oppressive aspects of life.

My father has been on assignment and called Xavier with a new rule recommendation for the game they have yet to fully explain to the rest of us. He hasn't done any more than send me a quick text to let me know he's alive, but Xavier says this new rule will completely alter the game experience, so I guess that's something.

Dean has a potential new client that sounds fascinating, though he doesn't have all the details yet. There's definitely an undercurrent of familiar peer pressure going on in this portion of the conversation. He's still hoping I will fully cut ties with the FBI and start a new career as a private investigator alongside him. I'll admit that was something I considered at one point. After Greg's death and not being able to figure it out, I felt like I'd had enough. I'd done all I could for the Bureau and needed something different in my life. Discovering my cousin and learning more about him gave me the idea of continuing to devote my life to helping others, just in a different context. I went so far as to take the classes and prepare for the test. But in the end, the Bureau still has its hold on me. Maybe one day. Just not now.

I check in about Ava. My mind still isn't fully made up as to whether I think my former supervisor at the Bureau assigned the brand-new agent to shadow me as a form of subtle psychological torture, or if there was a kernel of truth about him thinking it would be good for the young woman to see me in action at the beginning of her career.

Considering Creagan knew secrets about my mother's death and my family's connection to the tiny town of Feathered Nest, then used that information to throw me into the lion's den of a serial killer investigation, conspired for years with both Jonah and the drug lord called the Dragon, attempted to align himself with a cult called the Order of Prometheus, and then tied a pretty little bow on it all by trying to frame me for the brutal murder of my ex-boyfriend, I am more inclined to lean toward the former.

But regardless of why Aviva James ended up in my life, she did, and I had to learn nothing was going to change that. I won't pretend the start of our relationship was smooth and we immediately bonded. In fact, saying it was rocky from jump would be putting it very gently. But we figured ourselves out and came to an understanding that put us in a much better place.

Sharing near-death experiences will do that to you sometimes.

Her shadowing me was only ever meant to last for a short time, though, so after the last undercover assignment I brought her into resulted in the entire situation with Creagan, Jonah, and the Dragon blowing up, and our discovery of Xavier's crude but painfully effective fighting methods, she went on her way to start on her own path.

Since she was assigned to the field office near Harlan, she would be far closer to Dean and Xavier. They don't live in Harlan proper, but the suburb of Saltville is close enough I think of them as living there. It means they can stay in touch, and I know she has asked for their input on a couple of the cases she's worked since going off on her own.

It's good to know there's still a link. That there's someone else out there who has had the kinds of experiences we have. She may not have been around from the beginning, but she understands at least some of what we've gone through and it's good to have her in case we ever need to reach out to her.

Dean's eyelids are drooping before I realize how late it's gotten. I still feel awake as I help clean up the marshmallows, but that's not a surprise. I hoped coming here to stay for a few days might help me to relax more and break the insomnia cycle before it gets too deep, but I've learned not to expect sudden miracles. I'll give it a night and see what tomorrow brings.

I say goodnight to Dean and Xavier and get my bags to bring them to the guest room that's practically become a home away from home over the last couple years. I haven't set a specific end date to my stay and they haven't pushed me for one. My cousin has always said I'm welcome in his home the same way he's welcome in mine. Whenever and for however long.

I'm sure if he contextualized it in the same way, Xavier would agree. As it is, he likes when I show up and spending the extra time with me, but it's not a matter of welcoming me or giving me any kind of specific permission to stay for as long as I want to. By morning, me being here will just have become a part of his reality and he won't think much of it. As long as I don't interfere with his patterns and routines too much, it won't occur to him to wonder when I'm leaving any more than he would wonder when Dean was leaving.

In Xavier's mind, I will just be.

Sometimes, that's a very nice mode of existence. I don't have to be on guard or wonder what anyone is thinking. I don't have to feel constantly hyper-aware of my surroundings or what I'm doing. It means I can just be myself. Not Agent Emma Griffin, FBI Super Agent. Not Mrs. Emma Johnson, small-town celebrity.

Just Emma.

And sometimes it means I blend too much and don't get the kinds of warnings I probably should. Which is why an hour after everyone else went to bed and I'm trying to be as quiet as I can be making my way to the kitchen, a blast of cold air against my ankle and the feeling of something crawling up the back of my leg makes me jump, scream, and slam into the wall beside me.

This promptly causes the light fixture beside my head to pop on, nearly blinding me in the semi-darkness that had previously been only broken by moonlight coming in through the windows and the very occasional and seemingly haphazardly placed nightlights throughout the house. Of course, I know Xavier, which means there was nothing 'hap' about it. Right now, it's all about the hazard.

"Dammit, Xavier!" I grumble as I step back from the wall and try to rub some semblance of functioning into my eyes.

"I'm sorry."

I whip around and see Xavier standing at the edge of the living room.

"Holy hell, how long have you been standing there?" I ask.

"About ten seconds," he says. "I was in the kitchen when I heard my intruder alert system."

"Your what?"

"My intruder alert system. The cold air and pressure-activated light," he explains.

"Xavier," I say as calmly as I can, "you do realize an intruder alert system is supposed to let you know an intruder has come into the home, right? It's not meant to make the intruder more alert. This isn't a light lavender spritz in the face to keep them fresh through a night of robbery situation."

He nods. "I know."

"Then what's with the cold air on the ankle? I'm nowhere near the front door."

"You know I don't like the sound of alarms," he says. This is very true. I've seen him actively avoid touching any door or window when he just suspects there might be an alarm. He hates the sound so much that just the anticipation of it makes him unwilling to touch anything that could possibly create that reaction. "Besides, what if someone comes in through a different place in the house? Or they get in and then we can't find them?"

"So, your solution is shooting cold air at their ankles and making a light turn on if they happen to smack into the wall?"

"It's a fairly common reaction," he says.

I'm not sure I want to know about his field market research for that statement.

"So, your hope is that if someone is in this part of the house, they'll be hit by the cold air, smash into the wall, the light will turn on to make them visible, and you'll just happen to be standing there?" I raise an eyebrow.

"No," he says simply, shaking his head. "That's a lot of hypothetical variables. I figure they'll be hit by the cold air, fall over into the wall, and get startled enough for it to delay them until I can call the police. My watch tells me whenever the system is activated and there's a camera that starts recording as soon as the light turns on."

I look around but don't see the camera. All I can hope is that I'm not currently being live-streamed to a room full of police officers. I'm not even going to ask. That's not information I need to have in my head right now.

I walk past him on my continued way toward the kitchen.

"You made a lot of assumptions with that design, by the way," I say. "What if the person wasn't close enough to that part of the wall for the air to hit them? What if they are wearing long pants that mean they can't feel the air or the creepy-crawly feeling afterward? And what if they aren't all that surprised by it and don't hit the wall to turn the light on?"

He opens his mouth to start talking and I have a change of heart. "You know what? Don't tell me. I don't want to know. But do you think you could deactivate any of your other gadgets and gizmos around the house for while I'm here? Or at least tell me what to keep an eye out for?"

"I'm pretty sure I did," he says. I give him a withering look. "Not that one. I missed that one. But I know I deactivated other ones." He pauses and seems to think for a couple of seconds while I get down a mug for a glass of milk and a couple of cookies. "I'll check."

I nod. "I appreciate that. So, what are you doing up?"

"Feeding," he says with a sigh anyone who has ever spent time with a new mother would find familiar. "I'm in a critical phase with my new starters and they have to be fed on their regular schedule or they won't grow into their big, strong potentials."

"Of course," I mutter. "I figured you should have a new one by now."

"Not one," he says, going over to a pantry beside the refrigerator, reaching in, and coming out with an armful of three jars. He holds them out to me. "These were born on Halloween. I call them the Witches of Yeastwick."

CHAPTER SIX

"**D**ID I WAKE YOU?" ASKS SAM ON THE OTHER SIDE OF THE PHONE. I let out a little moan and rub my tired eyes, leaning back against the cushion of the recliner.

"I wish you did," I say. "I still can't sleep. What are you doing up so late?"

"Not up late," Sam counters. "Up early. It's almost sunrise."

I groan again and lean around to look out the window. It's still dark, but there's the line of softening light right on the edge of the horizon in the distance.

"Perfect. I've been up all night."

"You've just been sitting up alone?" he asks.

"Well, Xavier was up with me for a little while going over the genealogy of his starters. Apparently, some of them have gone off to neighbors and Dean's clients."

"He finally let them leave the nest? That's brave of him."

"I thought so. He does require them to send occasional updates and had Dean start him an Instagram for them to post pictures," I say.

"Oh, well. Yeah, that makes sense."

I sigh and launch myself up out of the chair so I can make my way into the kitchen to make coffee. It's already brewing when I walk into the room. The automatic coffeemaker may just be one of my top five favorite inventions from my lifetime.

"How is everything going there?" I ask. "Anything new?"

"No, unfortunately," Sam admits. "I honestly thought I was going to show up here and she would just kind of pop up. Part of me hoped she was off doing something and didn't think she needed to tell her mother where she was going because she's an adult. I had this idea she would somehow figure out that we were looking for her and come back, or would just finish up what she was doing and show back up and be embarrassed that there was all this fuss going on because of her."

"That's understandable," I nod. "It's not like Marie to do this. She hasn't ever just disappeared before, has she?"

I take a mug down out of the cabinet and fill it with coffee. The smell alone is enough to cut through some of the fog, but I know it's going to take a few of these to really perk me all the way back up. I need to sleep. I can't keep going like this.

"No," Sam replies. "She's always been really dependable. Even predictable. She's never just picked up and gone anywhere without telling somebody. It was never liked she called Aunt Rose every single day or anything, but this is just totally unlike her. She keeps in contact with people pretty well. Even as a kid, Marie was never the type to be spontaneous about things like going on vacation or taking a road trip. She wouldn't just toss everything in her car and leave without telling a friend or putting some sort of plans into place for it."

"Well, what about that? Do you know where her car is? Is a lot of her stuff gone?"

"Her car is missing," Sam tells me. "It hasn't been seen since she was last seen. We don't know about her stuff."

"What do you mean?" I ask. "Didn't her apartment either look like stuff was there or like it wasn't?"

"That's the thing," he explains. "We haven't been able to get into her apartment."

"Why not?" I raise an eyebrow. "Doesn't somebody have a key?"

"No," he says. "Apparently, Rose had one, but the landlord at Marie's building changed all of the locks recently. I thought it sounded pretty suspicious, but it's just something he does every year as a security measure. Marie meant to go get one of the new keys copied for her mother so somebody would have one in case of emergencies, but she hadn't gotten around to it yet."

"And the landlord won't let you in?" I ask.

"No," he says. "His stance is that Marie is an adult. She has the right to do anything she wants, go anywhere she wants, and disappear if she wants. She also has the right to privacy."

"That's true," I nod.

"Yeah, but it also means unless we can prove probable cause and show there is some sort of real reason to allow us access to her apartment, we're not going to be allowed to go in. And there could be evidence in there, something to tell us what happened and where she is."

I don't want to point out that it's possible Marie could be in there. Sam doesn't need to hear that right now.

"How about a welfare check?" I ask.

"I already tried that. Apparently, a woman not making contact with any of her family or friends in a couple of weeks isn't enough to justify it. The police department here isn't willing to enter her apartment without permission just on the off chance that there could be something in there that would tell us where she is. They say unless there is a true belief that she is in that apartment and in need of aid, or there is an imminent threat to her or to other people and entering the apartment to stop that threat, they have no grounds to enter."

"So, unless you figure something out, or for some reason, the landlord needs to get inside, there's no way that you can get in," I say.

"Exactly. So, right about now, I'm holding out for a gas leak. Or roaches."

"We can only hope," I sigh.

I start my second cup of coffee and start digging around in the kitchen for something to make for breakfast. Considering the timing on the coffeemaker, I assume the guys will be up soon and it would be nice to have something ready for them to eat. That and the marshmallows last night didn't exactly fill me with nutrition and were the only thing I ate since breakfast, so I am feeling a bit on the ravenous side.

"I really feel like we need to get in there," Sam says. "It's been too long, and we can't just pretend that this is normal anymore."

"They aren't pretending it's normal, Sam," I point out. "They called you to come and help them look for her. Obviously, your aunt knows something's going on."

"I know," he says. "But it almost seems like she's in denial about it."

"What do you mean?" I ask.

I hold the phone between my ear and my shoulder as I pick things out of the refrigerator and try to carry them all over to the counter without dropping anything.

"Aunt Rose is worried, but she keeps talking about Marie as if she did this on purpose. She told me she was being kind of secretive leading up to when she disappeared."

"What does she mean secretive?"

"I'm not sure," he sighs. "Just that she wasn't exactly acting like herself. She was still calling but wasn't giving as many details about what was going on in her life as she usually did. They had always had good communication before, but Marie started being vague. She wouldn't say what she was doing, just that she 'had stuff to do' or that she was 'busy'. If Rose asked her who she was going with or what she was doing, Marie would just sort of brush it off."

"Do you think she could have been in a relationship she doesn't want anybody to know about?" I ask.

I'm trying hard not to put myself in the mind space that will think of Marie as another case. It's not an official case yet, not until the police declare her missing and decide to actively pursue it. And even when it is, this is Sam's thing. I don't want him to feel like I'm interfering or stepping on his toes. He needs to be able to think through this and handle it his way, not with me chasing around after him trying to prod him along in the way that I would do it.

"It's possible," he admits. "I really don't know. It goes back to her being an adult, I guess. She could be seeing someone and not telling anybody, and that would be her right. She doesn't have to advertise every detail of her life and her relationships."

"Really?" I ask, taking down a mixing bowl. "I thought that was the whole point of social media."

He lets out a little bit of a laugh, making me smile. I love when he laughs.

"Alright, we all know how you feel about that whole situation. If I had to guess, I would say that is the most likely scenario. She is involved with someone and doesn't necessarily want to tell people about it yet."

"But?" I ask, noticing his hesitation.

He sighs. I never give him a break.

"But I don't understand why she would go off like this for so long if it was just that she's dating somebody and wanted to keep it to herself. I mean, I guess she could have run off and eloped."

"Sure, but eloping is usually just getting married without other people. Couples don't often have secret honeymoons that stretch on for weeks. What about her work? I know at the reception she said she was writing. Doing a blog of some kind? Am I remembering that correctly?"

"Yeah," Sam says. "She went to school for journalism but since she graduated a few years ago she hasn't really had a career. She's had different jobs, but nothing significant or long-lasting. She started the blog a few months ago and has been trying to monetize it. I guess she's kind of making a go of it."

"Have you checked the blog? Seen if it was updated or anything?" I offer.

"I have," he says. "I even took a page out of my wife's very thorough book and scoured through the comments on the posts to see if there was anything suspicious."

"Look at you," I grin. "FBI-ing it up."

"I don't know if I'd go that far, but it's a good tip."

"Not one that actually came up with anything, though, I'm guessing."

"Nope," he says. "She has some pretty avid readers, but I didn't get a kidnapper or killer vibe from any of them."

"That's encouraging," I note.

"The fewer of those vibes the better, generally," he says. "I just wish there was something more to go on."

"I know you do, babe," I say, aching for my husband. I know how hard this is for him and wish there was something more I could do.

"Well, I should probably get going," he says. "After breakfast, Rose and I are going out to do some more searching and then I'm going to talk to the department again to see if I can convince them to do something more. What are you up to today?"

"We're going back to Salvador's arena to do another search," I tell him. "Eric really wanted us to wait for him so that he could come with, and give us as much information as he can, but we just can't sit around and wait. There could be evidence that could get damaged or removed. The doctors still haven't released him from the hospital and the timeline got derailed because of an infection in one of his injuries, so we just have to go ahead with it. I'm going to do a video call with him while we're there to see if there's anything he can point out by looking at it that way."

"That's a good plan. I hope it goes well for you. I miss you."

"I miss you, too," I say.

I want to tell him I hope he comes home soon, but I stop myself.

Life in law enforcement, whether it's the FBI or as a sheriff, is stressful enough. I don't want to add more to it. I never want the obligations of our careers to cause any sort of strain or difficulty in our marriage. I ran from Sam when we were younger for that very reason. I didn't believe I could really give all of my focus to both, and I felt I was called to make the Bureau my priority.

Now I know I can have both, but it's not going to just fall into place. Especially in times when both my husband and I are working on cases that don't have anything to do with each other, we're going to have to make the effort to never make it seem like that choice is necessary.

And if it means at the end of the day still have each other, that effort is worth it.

CHAPTER SEVEN

Leftover signs of police activity at a crime scene can have one of two effects. Either it makes it more eerie and uncomfortable, underscoring that the place has been forever altered and will never again be what it once was, or it can have the opposite impact and actually take away from the intimidation and chill of a dark, disturbing place.

That's what's happened with the gladiator arena. The first time I came here, it was with my gun drawn, my heart in my throat, and beads of sweat running down my spine as I braced myself to rescue one of my best friends from the edge of death. The entire time we raced through traffic, following the tracking chip Xavier installed in Eric's watch and rushing into the building, all I could think about was the way Eric and I left things between us.

We've been friends a very long time and have seen each other through more than most people do in an entire lifetime. He's seen me at my worst and at my best, and I'd like to think the same for him. That means there were bound to be some moments of tension and conflict between us. People don't spend decades close to each other without occasionally getting tangled up in each other's hair to the point of driving each other right to the very edge.

But usually, that doesn't last long. Especially considering our high-stress jobs, the situations we've shared, and the fact that we both possess fairly intense personalities, we've actually had very few real fights. We've had some arguments that blew up, but were over within a day or two. We always were able to put it behind us. Nothing too serious. Nothing to hang onto.

But the conflict that came up between us this last time was something different. I don't even know how to describe it or how to explain why it affected me as much as it did. As soon as the words came out of his mouth, he knew he shouldn't have said them. His regret and immediate apology didn't mean anything to me, though. He'd said the words. They formed in his mind and came out of his mouth. Obviously, they meant something.

You are the reason Jonah is the way he is.

I'm never going to forget hearing him say that. Or the feeling that settled down into me as soon as I heard it. Not because it was some shocking, revolutionary concept that came out of nowhere. But because it was a deep pain I've been carrying around, dragging behind me and hoping it would eventually fall away. I've done everything I can to convince myself I'm not responsible for the horrors Jonah committed. That I don't need to share blame for the lives that were lost and destroyed.

But with that one sentence, a man who is supposed to be one of my very best friends, a member of my family, the partner of my other best friend, and the father to my godchild, confirmed the thing I have feared and hated most about myself.

That I am the reason he is what is.

Even before that, before I even knew that Jonah existed, I

grasped tight on the fear that I had somehow contributed to my mother's death. There was so much about it I didn't remember, and as I got older, I found out the memories I thought I had were wrong. It fills me with a sense of dread and guilt. Somehow, I had caused it. What I couldn't remember would hold the key to what really happened and what involvement in it I had.

It's not that I ever believed I killed her or that I knew it was going to happen. There was just the constant overhanging sense that I was somehow in the middle of it all. Now that I know what happened and why, that feeling hasn't gone away. And now, knowing so much more about the truth, the intangible sense of responsibility has become a feeling of being forced to hold that burden. It isn't mine. It was forced on me. But there's no way to escape it.

It's like when you skip a stone across the surface of the water. The stone is to blame for breaking the calm surface of the water, but it isn't to blame for being thrown.

I know that Jonah was always obsessed with my mother since he met her, and she fell in love with my father instead. He calls it love, but it's absorption. Enmeshment. He became completely wrapped up in her to the point that it became part of his identity, and his brain couldn't comprehend the possibility of having a future that didn't involve her.

My birth only made it worse. That's where my blame comes in. He thought I was his child. Seeing his twin brother raise me drove him mad, and he decided the only course of action was to take me away so he could be sure I was raised in the life he wanted me to have. That started a landslide of events that resulted in him being cut out of the family, my mother being murdered, my father going on the run with me, and people pledging their lives to service of a leader they believed would one day rule all of existence.

All the while, Jonah thought of only one thing. Me. Even when he was exiled and had to stay unseen beyond his most loyal followers so no one would know he was alive, he couldn't stop thinking about me. I represented something to him that to this day he can't stand. Something fuels his anger and heightens his desperation.

I am something he wants but that he can't have.

It's not that I think Jonah would have any chance of being normal no matter what. I hate to even use the word normal, but it's the only thing I can think of to say when I'm trying to describe him not being the way he is. I don't think he has the capacity to live life without the glory of his followers and the fulfillment of his delusions. Not life beyond bars, anyhow.

But he has escalated because of me. He kidnapped, tortured, and killed Greg because he was trying to get to me.

Hearing Eric put voice to that feeling was painful, but it also left me feeling like I couldn't even be angry with him. It was more a feeling of pain and betrayal. Like he had been feeling this way about me all the time and I never knew.

I couldn't bring myself to speak to him after that. The only words I exchanged with him were specifically about the case we were working on together. I didn't know if I would ever be able to see him in the same way.

And then I found out he'd come here. He offered himself up to the Emperor to help me. He risked his life and family, even with a baby at home, to make things right. And he was beaten bloody and nearly killed in this very gladiator cage for it. I was terrified we would never have the chance to make up. That the last days we were both on this Earth would be fractured.

But he survived. He pulled through the brutality and horror and is going to be alright. There's still a road ahead of him. He still has to overcome quite a bit of damage before he's going to be back to his old self, but it's going to come. And everything else is behind us.

Except for this place. I won't put it behind me until it's given up every one of its secrets. Exhausted though I might be, I won't rest until I can at least get some semblance of justice for the victims who suffered and died here. And that starts with going over every inch of it, looking at it from every angle, and forcing it to tell us everything it has to tell.

Police floodlights, bright yellow crime scene tape draped around specific spots, various colors of flags sticking up out of the ground, and the constant chatter of voices filling it up has taken the power away from the arena. It isn't foreboding anymore. It's cowering now.

This space used to be treated almost like a temple. There were clear-cut spaces belonging to the different types of people who entered it. The tight hallways for the masked man who transported the fighters. The cells that held the men waiting in fearful trepidation before they fought—and those lucky, or unlucky, enough to survive. The bloody dirt-floored arena littered with weapons and random implements meant to turn into weaponry with as much brutality and creativity as the fighters could channel.

And the shadowy balcony where the Emperor oversaw it all.

It's grotesque and impressive at the same time. The attention to detail is staggering and especially after seeing it, it's difficult to wrap my head around the fact that it's here and yet no one noticed it. How did this place even come into existence? Who built something like this underground without questioning its purpose?

But now so much of that mystique and brutality has been stripped away. It's laid bare in the bright illumination of the lights and the unflinching examination by the detectives. And me. I won't let them be the only ones to scour the layers and tear them apart bit by bit until this place is reduced to concept.

Salvador Marini killed in several states. He kidnapped and tortured women and men. He drugged his victims and I have absolutely no doubt he was no stranger to the weapons black market. That makes his case the domain of the Bureau. The police already involved in Serena's murder and Dean's attack are a part of the investigation, and the resources of the local departments in all areas affected by the Emperor are cooperating. But the FBI became involved immediately and Eric himself assigned me to the case.

I appreciate all the manpower I can get. This case is extensive and complicated, and I have the sinking feeling in my gut we don't even know the full extent of it. There will be more victims. There will be people Salvador brought in to help him and then got rid of. There will be more arenas, more dump sites.

And I'll dismantle them all.

"Any indication of how many men were brought through here?" I ask Detective Noah White.

The Harlan police department is working in cooperation with the local department to further intensify the investigation. Dean was abducted from Noah's jurisdiction and brought to this arena. The two locations are so close it's very likely more victims came from the area as well. Noah is trying to help make these connections and provide an understanding of the Harlan area to give more context to the arena and the victims chosen.

It's good to see familiar faces at investigations that are this personal. I like knowing I'm not the only one with more of a stake than just professional interest. I know Noah doesn't have the depth of personal investment that I do, but he knows me, he knows Dean. He knows Xavier and Sam. He's heard me talk about Eric and Bellamy. And Jonah. This brings the whole case closer to home for him.

"No," Noah shakes his head. "It's obvious there were quite a few over some time, but we haven't found any specific records or anything yet."

I nod. "I doubt we're going to find anything written out to say who was here and what was done to them. That would be too humanizing. We just need to make sure we gather every bit of information and evidence we can possibly find. Search everywhere, see if there are any indications of other places where he might have done the same thing."

"You really do think there are other arenas like this around?" he asks.

"I know there are," I say. "Not many, though. It would be far too difficult to pull off having things like this planned and built a whole bunch of times without somebody saying something about it. Which means there's something important about this area. He chose this spot specifically for a reason. If we can figure out that reason, we might be able to identify the other locations and maybe find more victims."

"Here's hoping," he replies. "Or actually, not hoping. Here's hoping there are no other places like this after all."

"I'll drink to that."

CHAPTER EIGHT

*E*MMA IS LOOKING FOR YOU.

There has to be some better way for me to get in touch with Jonah, but he won't give me a phone number to call him or any email address to send messages. The only way I can reach out to him is to leave the cryptic comment on a specific article and wait for him to get in touch with me from a blocked number. At this point, I've used several different fake names and accounts to leave the message. I'm trying to minimize how suspicious and strange it looks.

But no matter how many times I mention it to him, he won't change the system. I try not to let myself dwell on how much it feels like just another way he's trying to control me. He knows he can't manipulate me the way he does other people. He's never going to earn my loyalty or devotion. I will never be committed to him the way his followers have been. So, to ease his own mind, he has to find ways he can still exert that control.

I only have to wait a few minutes before my phone rings and yet another unknown number flashes across the screen. I don't know if he's using technology that changes the phone number every time he calls or is constantly trading out burner phones. Either way, it's been impossible to track him.

"I want to know more about the Emperor," I start.

"What do you want to know?"

"Anything you have to tell me," I say. "I need to know who he was and what brought him to the place where he started doing these things to other people."

"I can't tell you all of that," Jonah says. "I don't know what made him do what he did. I know what he said was his reason, that he felt above other people. That he deserved the indulgences and entertainment. That the gods had favored him. But he and I weren't friends, Emma. I didn't know him well. Remember, he was not part of Leviathan. He was being used by Leviathan."

"I know," I nod. "But why? He wasn't that big of a deal. Yes, he had money. And he was clearly able to charm and manipulate people. But why him? Why did Serena make him her primary target?"

"For me," he says.

"What do you mean?"

"I gave her Miley Stanford's life. I made sure she was able to step right into it and that she wouldn't be questioned."

"So, she repaid you by becoming an accomplice for a serial killer?" I raise an eyebrow. "I don't understand."

"I don't expect you to," he replies. "I didn't know what he was doing. Not to the extent that she was."

"I just don't get the link to Miley. I know you felt like you needed to protect Serena from her family, but why did that mean putting her into the life of a missing girl? Is Miley really missing?"

"I don't know where she is," he says.

"But do you know what happened to her?"

"No."

"Who was she, Jonah? What does she have to do with any of this?" I ask.

"She was exactly who she was." He's starting to sound on edge. Aggravated. "A young woman who was lost."

"Did you lose her?" I ask.

"Yes." It's a chilling response that makes my spine tighten. "I didn't kill her. But I lost her."

"Salvador Marini referred to Serena as Miley. He thought that was her real name. He wouldn't have done that if he'd killed Miley or took her in some way."

"Do you know the first thought I had when I found out how he died?

"Salvador?" I ask.

"Yes. When I found out what happened, the first thing that went through my head was what poetic justice it was. This man never did anything by himself. There were always people around him to fawn on him. To help him."

"But he died alone of a heart attack," I say.

Jonah makes a sound in the back of his throat like he's making an acknowledgment, giving me my own space to contemplate the meaning of how Salvador died.

"It was his last morning of freedom. It would have felt so strange for him to face it on his own," Jonah says.

∽

"The wording of it didn't sit right with me," I tell Xavier that night as we sit in front of the fireplace again. This time a spread of different candy bars left over from Halloween sits on the rug with us and he's pre-broken what looks like several boxes of graham crackers into squares. "He didn't say it had to be strange or that it was strange. He said it would have *felt* so strange."

"Like it was hypothetical," Xavier says.

"Exactly."

"Do you think he killed him?"

"No," I say. "Usually when it comes to Jonah, there's always that possibility, but I really don't think so with him. Not the way he reacted when I told him Salvador was dead. And what benefit would it be for him to pretend he didn't have anything to do with it? He's already on the run, I can't catch him. What's the benefit of hiding it? I have no doubt I will get him, but even if he was brought to trial for another murder, why would it matter? And he was adamant about not being responsible for Serena's death. He was very open about the other things that he's done and willing to give details about his other crimes.

"It just doesn't make any sense that he would cover this one up and let me keep investigating it. If he killed Salvador because Salvador killed Serena, he would just tell me. It would be over and we wouldn't have to keep looking into it. But when I said the situation was over, he said it wasn't. That we still had to figure out what happened to Miley Stanford.

"I still don't understand what Salvador could have had to do with Miley's disappearance, but there's a link there and Jonah wouldn't cut off a source of information about her." I shake my head as I construct a fairly epic peanut butter cup s'more. "No. He didn't kill him."

"But you still don't think it was just a heart attack."

"I don't know what to think." I look over at him and see him carefully arranging chocolate kisses on one of his graham crackers. "You're just going to use those?"

"Yes," he says. He takes the toasted marshmallow he had carefully leaned against the hearth and positions it on top of the chocolate, sliding it into place with the top cracker.

"You know that's just a regular s'more."

"Regular ones are made with bars," he counters.

"It's the same chocolate."

"The shape changes the mouthfeel and the flavor experience."

"It melts," I say. "It's all in the shape of a puddle by the time it gets to your mouth."

"It's different," he insists.

"Hey, Emma," Dean calls from outside the room.

"In here," I say.

I get to my feet, licking melted chocolate and crushed peanut butter filling off my fingers. He comes in carrying my phone. He looks down at Xavier.

"Fancy s'mores today," he notes.

"It's a chocolate kiss," I say quietly. "It's literally the exact same chocolate."

"Different shape creates a different flavor experience. It's all in the mouthfeel."

"So I've heard," I say. "What's up?"

"Oh, your phone was ringing. You left it in the kitchen. It rang a few times. It was..." As he says it, the phone starts ringing again and we both look at the screen, "Bellamy."

I gingerly take the phone, trying not to smear it with any of my s'more goo, and answer it.

"B?"

"Emma," she starts. I can hear the tears in her voice. Something is wrong. "I've been trying to call you."

"I'm sorry, I left my phone in the other room. What's going on? What's wrong?"

Dean looks at me through narrowed eyes, his eyebrows pulled together curiously. I shake my head slightly, shrugging to let him know I don't know why she's upset.

"Are you still at Dean and Xavier's house?" Bellamy asks.

"Yeah. I'm going to be here for a few days at least. Why?"

"I need you."

"Bellamy, what is going on?"

I make my way toward the kitchen to wash my hands.

"Liza Fielding is dead."

CHAPTER NINE

"Liza Fielding?"

I know I've heard the name. It's familiar in the kind of way that I know I've heard it and probably said it, but I can't place it.

"My sorority sister back at U of A," Bellamy explains. "She got married a few years ago in the vineyard."

"And you had to wear the mauve bridesmaid dress you said made you feel like Minerva. I remember. She's a lawyer, right?"

"She has a family law firm," Bellamy says, then lets out a sob. "She's gone."

"What happened?" I ask as the effort of trying to remember her dissipates and the reality of the news sinks in.

"I'm not sure. Her husband just called. Emma, I have to go up there."

"Of course," I say. "Do you want me to take care of Bebe while you're gone? I know Eric isn't going to be discharged yet."

"No," she says. "I want you to come with me."

"Come with you?"

I'm trying not to sound surprised by the request. She's in a really cold, horrible place right now and I don't want to cause her any more upset. But I don't know any of her sorority friends. I've encountered them here and there over the years, but I never made friends with any of them. It isn't that I disliked them offhand or specifically didn't want to be friends with them. It's just that her sorority was a separate world from me, even back in college. It was something that was Bellamy's and I left her to it.

I didn't fit in in that world and, to be honest, never really tried. I didn't have any interest in it. There was too much else for me to be focused on, and I didn't see myself as having anything in common with those women. I can look back on that time of my life now and know I wasn't open to anything. It was one of the most closed and hardened times in my life. The fact that B stuck with me throughout it all is a testament to her, not to me.

But even without knowing the women or having anything to do with them, I know how much they've meant to Bellamy. Over the years she's been in their weddings and celebrated their careers. Some of them have gone on to have children and move to other parts of the country or the world. Others have stayed right in the same area, but largely put the years of the sorority and college behind them, settling for a quick Christmas newsletter each year and an appearance at the reunions every few.

Liza was a part of a much closer group that has stayed tight-knit over the years. Of them, Bellamy was the only one to have found a partner who wasn't a part of their circle in college and the first to have had a child. And now, one of them is gone.

"Yes. Would you come? I know you're busy and you have all these cases going..."

"B, that doesn't matter. The investigations are being handled. If you need me, I can take a couple of days away from them," I tell her.

"I do," she says. "I need you. I know you don't really know them, but you're my best friend and I can't do this without you. Especially since I can't have Eric there with me, either."

"I understand. Just let me know what I need and when to be ready," I say.

When I get off the phone with Bellamy, I call Sam to tell him what's going on. I don't really expect him to answer, but he does. I hesitate slightly when I tell him, knowing he asked me to go with him to find out what was going on with his cousin, and I told him I couldn't go because I was too busy with work, but am going with Bellamy.

I don't want his feelings to be hurt, or for him to think I don't care as much about what's going on with him. But my worries are put to rest in an instant. He understands immediately. My cases have shifted since he left to see his family, and since his visit up to Michigan was more open-ended, it's easier for me to be able to commit to supporting Bellamy through the extremely hard days immediately following her friend's death.

For what feels like the millionth time already in my marriage, and what I know will not be the last, I think of how amazing my husband is.

"Tell her I'm thinking about her," he says. "And give me a call when you can."

"I will," I say. "Thank you."

He lets out a little laugh. "For what?"

"For being you."

"Has Xavier started making you watch that women's network Thanksgiving movies so he can make his yearly attempt to understand them beyond their inherent flaws and derivative plot concepts again?"

I can almost hear the words in Xavier's voice.

"Yes," I confirm. "But thank you anyway."

Sam chuckles. "You're welcome. You go on and get ready. Tell B I'm sorry. I love you."

"I love you, too."

"Is this where the dramatic music comes in?"

"Goodnight, Sam."

⁂

Bellamy gets to the house early the next morning. Her eyes are red and puffy, and she has that expression of confusion and disorientation that seems to come along with sudden death.

"Where's the baby?" I ask when I notice she hasn't carried in her year-old daughter, Emmabelle. I might never get over the honor that B bestowed upon me by naming her after me.

"I called Eric's mother and she came to watch the house and take care of the baby while I'm gone. Thank you for doing this," she explains.

"Of course. I would do anything for you. You know that."

I wrap her into a hug and feel her shaking in my arms. Dean comes into the room behind us and Bellamy steps away to accept a hug from him as well.

"I'm so sorry to hear about your friend," he says. "Do they know what happened?"

Bellamy shakes her head and brushes the tears away from her cheeks. "She just got really sick all of a sudden. Her husband said she was feeling a little off and said she was going to lie down. He didn't think a lot of it because of the time of year. It seems like most people are getting sick around now. But then she started throwing up and it got really bad, really fast. He got her to the hospital, but there was nothing they could do. They were trying to figure out what was going on and she flatlined. They couldn't bring her back."

A fresh tear slides out of her eye and she lets it fall to her shirt.

"I'm so sorry."

She nods. "Thank you." She lets out a breath and looks at me. "Are you ready? I just want to get there and get this over with."

"Sure," I nod. "I'm just going to tell Xavier I'm leaving."

I go into the small library where Xavier has taken up residence on a window seat and tell him I'll be gone for a couple of days.

"Are you going to her funeral?" he asks.

It might be a strange question coming from anyone else, but I'm very used to Xavier trying to find his way and put everything that happens into context. He has a difficult time grasping a reality that isn't happening right in front of him and needs specifics to understand what's happening.

"I don't know if there's going to be a funeral yet," I say. "This all just happened and it took everybody by surprise. I think for right now we're just going so that Bellamy can see her other friends and show some support to her husband. They might make further plans while we're there."

"You don't do funerals," he points out.

"I know," I say.

I've been to very few funerals in my life. I know some people find a tremendous amount of meaning in funerals. They appreciate the ritual and it's comforting to them to get together with other people for structured mourning. Deaths like Liza's, are often described as sudden. There wasn't a drawn-out time of preparation, like a serious illness or the process of old age—but the reality is all death is sudden. It's shocking to internalize the shift of living to no longer living even when you feel like you're ready for it.

A funeral can help with that. It eases the starkness of death and turns it into a transition, smoothing out the process so it feels more like the person has been ushered forward and less like they've just been plucked away.

But a funeral is for the living, not for the dead. It can be extremely helpful for some, but I'm not one of them. I would rather celebrate their life, then pay my respects on my own time with a visit to the grave or quiet time on my own.

It might be different for someone I don't know well. I've attended wakes for the victims of crimes I investigated so that I could show my support for the people I got to know during the investigation. In this situation, I will do whatever I need to do for Bellamy. This has obviously hit her hard and I want to make it easier in any way I can.

After all we've been through, thick and thin, it's the least I can do for her.

CHAPTER TEN

The drive up to the University of Alexandria takes a couple of hours and Bellamy is silent the entire time. She's lost in her thoughts, staring out the windshield as I drive. A couple of times I notice her look up into the rearview mirror as if she's trying to check on Bebe. It's like she's gone into survival mode and is just going through the motions.

It's the earliest stage immediately after finding out that someone has died. It seems trite to refer to it as shock, but that's really what it is. When you first hear that kind of news, it doesn't totally sink in. it just sits there on the brain, trying to find its way past all the expectations and concrete thoughts. Then it moves in deeper and starts the harder work of reprogramming.

It's the kind of news that doesn't add to your understanding of the world and your place in it, but takes away from it. As the knowledge of a person's death settles further in, it has to change existing plans, take away thoughts that automatically come to mind when thinking of that person, and make changes to those that will still come but need to be different.

It's not just as easy as thinking about not seeing that person anymore and the immediate impact. It's the days afterward. The times you hear something that reminds you of something you wanted to tell them and try to call. Or weeks later, when their birthday is coming up and you try to think of what you should get them. Or months later, when a holiday arrives that you've always spent with them, and you don't have any plans. Or years later, when a wedding or a baby or a graduation or a vacation happens, and you know every picture that's going to be taken will be missing someone.

That's the shock that hits. It's what Bellamy is going through now. Her mind is trying to unravel the bits that just assumed Liza would be on her Christmas card list or would call on her birthday or be at the next sorority reunion. Her mind is working too hard thinking through those. It can't focus on anything else.

I'm alright with that. In a way, I think that's why I'm here. She's relying on me to be the part of her thought process she doesn't really have touch with right now.

I'm not going to say it to her, but I know she's not just processing the emotions of Liza's death. She has done an incredible job staying strong throughout everything with Eric. She's cried and she's worried, but she hasn't really let herself fall apart and feel everything that should come along with getting so close to losing your partner.

Seeing her go through that would be too hard for Eric, and she knows that. She doesn't want him to worry about her while she's worried about him because it could make everything worse. He can't heal if he's focused on not wanting her to be upset about what he's going through.

This situation has given her permission to feel everything she's been trying not to feel.

We stop at our hotel first to drop off our bags and let Bellamy freshen up a little before heading over to the sorority house. It's located in one of the several historic neighborhoods surrounding the campus itself. The rest of the street looks quiet in the early afternoon sunlight. Thanksgiving isn't for another couple of weeks, so classes are still in session. At this time of day, these houses are generally empty, but they will come alive in the evening.

Bellamy's sorority didn't do a lot of partying in our time at school. I don't know if that's changed, but I doubt it. This organization has a long history and deep-rooted tradition. It's unlikely they would completely alter how they operate in such a relatively short time.

There's more activity as we get closer to the house. Women from young teens up through a generation or two older than us are scattered across the lawn and on the wide wraparound porch of the stately building. This house has been standing on this street for far longer than the school has been. It was once the elegant home of an extremely wealthy family who passed ownership of it to the matriarch's beloved sorority on her death. It's a beautiful home that's been kept immaculate for decades and provides a source of great pride to the sisters who call it home.

Bellamy didn't live in the house for the whole time she was in the sorority, but she loved the time she was there. She lets out a heavy sigh as we drive past in search of a parking spot. There's a lot of emotion in that sigh. It's sadness and longing. Nostalgia and comfort. Dread.

There are so many cars lining the street that we have to go up several blocks and down to another street. We finally find a spot and I revive my parallel parking skills to fit into it. It's probably not big enough and I should find another one, but that's not happening. The back tires of my car are already in it. I'm committed.

"Do you remember the first time I tried to parallel park?" Bellamy asks.

Her voice is so soft and powdery it takes a second to process the words. I nod.

"I'll never forget it," I chuckle. "You panicked partway through, got out of the car, and yelled at it."

A weak smile tugs up the corners of her lips briefly. "The neighbor called the police."

"I really think that officer thought one of us was trying to steal the car," I say. "He just couldn't figure out why."

"Or how we got the keys."

"But I took over and got us in," I point out, inching my car into the tight spot. "And we practiced with you for the rest of the semester."

"I still can't parallel park," she sighs.

"I know." She's still staring through the windshield and we sit quietly for a couple of seconds. "Are you ready?"

Bellamy nods. "Yeah. Let's go."

We walk down the sidewalk to join the sorority sisters and other friends gathered around the house. It's both a sobering and uplifting sight. I doubt most of these women know each other. The older ones have been away from campus for decades at this point and some of the younger ones are still in process of pledging. Yet, they're all gathered to remember Liza. Just being in the same space together is helping them get through.

As soon as we walk onto the lawn, a woman on the porch comes down the steps toward Bellamy and scoops her into a tight hug. The embrace brings both of them back to tears, but they rebound quickly and step apart.

"Emma, I don't know if you remember Regan Hall?"

"I think we met once," I say, nodding toward the dark-haired woman.

I start to say it's nice to see her but stop the platitude while the words are still hovering on my lips. It's not actually nice to see her. I don't know her and the only reason we're seeing each other is because a friend she shares with my best friend is dead. This is not the time or place for compulsive language.

"Are the others here?" Bellamy asks.

Regan nods. "They're inside. Liza was still really involved, so the sisters wanted to pay tribute to her. They wanted to make a place where people who knew and loved her could come and mourn."

"That's beautiful," Bellamy says.

We go into the house and Regan guides us into a parlor. Several pictures of Liza are set up around the room and a large book is open on a table, welcoming people to sign and share stories of her.

"There's Finn," Regan says, gesturing toward a man sitting on a couch near the book.

He looks distraught and I recognize him from pictures as Liza's husband. It strikes me as strange that he's here. His wife died only yesterday. There are so many other places I would think he should be than her old sorority house. But there are several people around him obviously supporting him, so maybe this is the best place for him. Anything that will give him comfort right now.

Bellamy brings me over to the group and gives hugs all around before introducing me. I meet Finn and give him an empathetic handshake. Bellamy introduces me to Adam, a college friend of theirs whose eyes seem an almost inhuman shade of blue from crying, Priscilla, a tiny, willowy woman who barely even looks at me, Darren, a big man who can't seem to stay sitting for more than a few seconds, and Maya, a woman who I recognize from the pictures from Liza and Finn's wedding. They're all either sitting on or standing near the couch, holding hands or wrapping their arms around each other. There's strength in the group. That's why Finn's here. He needs to be near all of them.

They greet me much like I expect them to. Not with outright dismissal or the feeling that they didn't want me around, but with hesitation. We all know of each other and we have Bellamy in common, but this isn't a cocktail party. It isn't a casual gathering of friends that could act as a convenient time to throw a new one into the deep end and hope the whole group gels.

I'm an outsider watching them grieve.

But I'm here for Bellamy, and that's all that matters to me. We stay at the sorority house for few hours listening to people share stories and memories of Liza. I stay as close to the wall as I can without actually climbing behind the couch, not wanting to get swept up into the greetings and hugs of condolence. I feel useful only when the occasional gawker starts asking questions they shouldn't be asking a widower who is less than forty-eight hours removed from his wife's death.

That's when I jump in to detour the conversation with stories from my career or anecdotes about Bellamy, shifting the attention away from Finn so he doesn't have to put his pain on repeat.

Finally, the crowd lessens and Adam pats Finn on the back.

"Why don't we go get something to eat? I know you haven't had anything all day."

"I'm not really hungry," Finn mutters.

"I know. But you still need to eat. Come on. Let's go to Murphy's."

There's something we have in common. That little diner played host to many of my favorite memories from my time at school as I'm sure it does for a lot of the students who come through here. It's one of those shared threads that transcends so many things about each of the individual students to make a connection throughout the university.

We take several cars and meet up at the diner. Waves of memories come over me as we step into the smell of biscuits and bacon and the sound of the jukebox playing on one side. The energy in the group shifts as we sit down and order drinks. Most of us order coffee, but a couple decide to channel their youth and choose to get their caffeine hit from sodas instead.

"How's Emmabelle?" Priscilla asks quietly as she stirs an alarming number of artificial sweetener packets into her coffee. "She must be getting big."

Bellamy nods and takes out her phone to show off pictures of Bebe. Eric's time in the Bureau, particularly his specialty handling cybercrimes and computer forensics, made him adamant about a couple of things when he became a father. One being that his daughter's face would never be shown on any kind of social media. Since Bellamy is one of the seemingly few people who mercifully hates the cheesy trend of sticking emojis over children's faces in a bid to at once show off and be secretive, the only parts of the baby that have ever been featured on her platforms are her feet and the back of her head.

"She is," B agrees. "I can't believe she's almost a year and a half old. It doesn't seem possible."

Suddenly, Maya sits up straighter and points at me. "Oh. Emma. The baby is named after you."

I offer a closed-lipped smile and nod as Bellamy puts her phone away.

"Yep," she smiles. She points at me. "Emma," then points at herself, "Belle. Emmabelle. But we call her Bebe."

The waitress comes by again to take our orders and as she walks away, the conversation melts into reminiscing about college days. They laugh at the same things and finish each other's sentences. I watch them. That's enough of a revisit to my college years for me. Learning to watch.

"So, Emma," Regan comments as we're eating and they've just finished laughing over a story that was broken down to its essential elements and delivered in mostly unlinked words and a few sound effects. "What's your story?"

I'm not sure where she's going with that. It's nice to see that they're able to redirect their grief and give Finn a boost talking about better times, but I don't know when I became an important part of the narrative.

"My story?" I raise an eyebrow. "Like I was born on a snowy Midwest winter night?"

Bellamy shakes her head through a swallow of her coffee. "You were born in Virginia in the middle of July."

"That doesn't make as good a story," I point out.

"That's not what I meant," Regan says. "It's just…" she looks around at the others, "we all know each other and spent a lot of time together in college. We've heard of you, obviously, but you weren't around much. Not the sorority type?"

"Regan," Priscilla whispers under her breath.

"It's fine," I say, looking at her, then back at Regan. "You can say that. I didn't do the sorority thing in college. I was distracted by my mother's unsolved murder and my father's disappearance, and debating whether I should continue to study painting or become an agent in the FBI. Turns out shooting Jell-o shots and shooting guns aren't recommended as part of the same program of study."

CHAPTER ELEVEN

"I'm sorry. I shouldn't have said that. It was really uncalled for," I say.

Bellamy shakes her head. "It's fine."

"No, it's not," I say. We're back at the hotel and B hasn't said more than five words since we got the check at the diner and left. "Emotions are really high right now and I shouldn't have snapped at her like that. She was just really…"

"Bitchy?" Bellamy completes my thought, turning away from going through her suitcase in search of some specific article of clothing. "It's okay. You can say it. She is. Regan has always been a tough one. She likes to belittle people."

"I noticed that."

"The Jell-o shots thing was a little bit off. We didn't party. Well, the sorority didn't. Regan did."

We laugh.

"Alright, well then I read her correctly. Still shouldn't have said it. I know this is really hard for all of you. Especially Finn. He's dealing with his wife dying. I shouldn't be causing conflict with his friends," I say.

"You know what?" Bellamy asks. "I think he actually liked it. Liza had a spark like you. It was probably good for him to hear someone else stand up to Regan. I'm sorry if you were really uncomfortable. I know we were sharing a lot of stories and things you don't know about."

"It's fine," I brush her off. "Xavier never knows what's going on. I'll just consider it a submersion course in how he thinks."

Bellamy shakes her head. "I don't think that can be translated into a seminar."

She finds the baggy shirt she was looking for and strips down before dropping it over her head.

"Alright, I have to know," I say. "When you were all doing your walk down memory lane, Maya said something about Finn making money when he started dating Liza. Everybody was laughing about it. Adam said he was working at a bank? I don't think I'm fully understanding the joke. Or partially understanding, for that matter. Is he bad at math? A mime now? What's funny?"

"He wasn't working there," Bellamy says. "He was just making regular visits and bringing home some cash afterward."

"Are you trying to not tell me that Finn robbed banks?" I raise an eyebrow.

"No, I'm trying to not tell you that Finn donated to a sperm bank."

I stare at Bellamy for a few seconds, waiting to see if she's going to laugh or tell me she's joking. She doesn't. Which makes me assume she's not.

"Well, thank you for not telling me that over dinner," I say.

She laughs. "It's always been one of Adam's favorite things to tease him about."

"I mean, was it seriously like a regular form of income for him? I'm not fully schooled in the guidelines or anything, but I thought this was more of a blood donation type situation," I say.

Bellamy shakes her head and climbs onto the other bed, picking up the drink she'd set on the bedside table and taking a sip.

"Nope, it actually does pay. Not a ton or anything, but some places pay about $100 for each donation. And if the guy is really qualified, he's asked to visit a few times a week."

"Qualified... to make the donation?"

"Good genes. Attractive. Smart. No scary disorders or chronic health issues. That kind of thing."

"OK, that's a different kind of qualification than I was thinking, but it makes a lot more sense." I think about this for a second. "Wow. Well, the things you learn. I didn't necessarily need for that to be one of them, but I know it now."

She holds up her drink like she's toasting me. "You're welcome."

"You look like you're pretty well settled in for the evening," I say.

She nods. "I just feel like hiding out here and not really thinking of anything for a while. I'm not looking forward to seeing everybody again tomorrow. That sounds awful, but this is just not the way that I want to reunite with them."

"It doesn't sound awful. It's completely understandable. This isn't a fun situation. But I know Finn is glad you're all here for him," I say.

"He's at a complete loss about what to do. She didn't have a health directive or an end-of-life plan. They hadn't even made a will yet," Bellamy says.

I look at her in shock. "Are you serious? She didn't need any of those plans?"

"She was only in her thirties," Bellamy points out.

"I'm aware of that," I say. "I'm only in my thirties. So are you and Eric and Sam. I know all of my end-of-life wishes are recorded and made very clear. So are Sam's. We have wills and health directives. Power of attorney for each other. Don't you and Eric have your plans in place?"

"Of course we do. But you and Eric and I are in the FBI. And Sam's a sheriff. We might not like to talk about it, but the reality is we are far more likely to need those plans earlier in our lives than people who own their own little businesses or are lawyers or other conventional jobs. The vast majority of the time people aren't pointing guns at the local CPA," she says.

"I mean, sometimes they do," I counter.

"Yes, and when they do, who are the people who come in and try to stop them from actually shooting said CPA? You and Eric and Sam. I don't go out in the field, so I'm not as much at risk, but it's still a hell of a lot more likely that one of us is going to need to know things like funeral songs and which charities to donate money to in lieu of flowers than it would be for any of them." Her sadness seems to have turned into frustration, but when it reaches its peak, it crashes back down into grief again. She hangs her head. "It's just not fair. It doesn't make sense."

"I know," I say, moving over to sit on the bed beside her. "I know it doesn't."

"Things like this shouldn't happen," she says. "Liza was fine. At least, we all thought so. She didn't tell anybody she was sick."

"Maybe she didn't know," I offer. "But you said it came on very suddenly."

She nods, her head dropping back to lean on the headboard. "Finn said she just wasn't feeling well and then it got worse. It was only a few hours between her symptoms first starting and them letting her go. I just don't even understand what that could be. How could it happen so fast?"

"I don't know," I say, wrapping my arm around her. "But they'll figure it out. I'm sure they'll do an autopsy and at least then you'll get some answers."

Bellamy shakes her head. "No."

I can't even begin to pretend I'm not shocked by that.

"No?" I ask. "She's not going to have an autopsy?"

"No," Bellamy says. "Not unless it's forced by the police, but there's no reason to. Unless the police are involved…"

I nod, knowing already what she's going to say. "Unless the police are involved, in Virginia it's not legally required to have an autopsy. It's up to the next of kin to give authorization after a death that isn't considered suspicious."

"Right," Bellamy nods. "And Finn doesn't believe in autopsies."

I pull away from her and give her an incredulous look. "He doesn't believe in autopsies? How do you not believe in autopsies?"

"Everybody has their own perspectives, Emma. They see death and the process surrounding it in their own way."

I shake my head. "This is a scientific procedure. It's critical to understanding how someone died and why. And he's talking about it like fucking fairies."

"He says he can't stand the idea of doctors defiling Liza's body. He just can't take the thought of them cutting her open and taking out her organs and prodding at her," Bellamy says.

"He doesn't need to pop popcorn and watch," I say. "But he should get the answers."

"I agree, but it's up to him. It's his right as her husband not to allow it, and that's what he's doing."

I'm baffled by the decision. The thought of simply accepting the death of someone you love when there seems to be no explanation is beyond me.

"God forbid anything like this ever happened to Sam, there's no way I would just sit by. I would need to know what happened to him. I couldn't just let him go without some explanation," I say.

"Not everybody feels that way, Emma. To Finn, it doesn't matter if he knows what killed Liza. She's still dead. Finding out what killed her isn't going to bring her back. It's not going to change the reality he's living in now. And it might even make it worse. He'd rather move forward."

I get up and stuff my feet into my shoes. "Since we're going to stay in for the rest of the evening, I'm going to go down to the front desk and see if they have any recommendations for good places to order in from around here. A lot has changed since the good old days."

She nods and I leave, sliding my key card into my pocket as I go. I am going to get the information from the front desk, but I'm really leaving the room to call Sam. I need to hear his voice.

∽

"She died under suspicious circumstances, and they aren't requiring an autopsy?" he asks after I've explained the situation.

"No," I tell him. "Apparently, they don't consider her death suspicious. They're calling it natural causes for right now. She just got really sick and they couldn't save her. But there wasn't anything to indicate it was anything else, so there isn't an investigation, and they can't legally require an autopsy."

"Well, I don't think this will actually make you feel any better, but I have some good news on my front," he says.

"Your front is always good news," I crack.

"Awwww, you managed a dirty joke even while you're angry at people who don't think the same way you do. That's my girl," he chuckles.

"Thanks. So, what is it? What's your good news?"

"We did a canvass of the neighborhood and one of Marie's neighbors suggested we talk to Marie's boyfriend since he was at the apartment just a few days ago," he says.

At first, this doesn't sound like anything but a really obvious next step in an investigation. Then I realize what he's saying.

"Her boyfriend?" I ask. "I thought you said she wasn't seeing anyone as far as you knew."

"She wasn't," Sam says. "And none of her friends could think of a man she would be seeing. They say she didn't mention anything to them or give any indication that she was even thinking about dating anyone."

"But there was a man at her apartment a few days ago?" I ask.

"Apparently someone in the next building over stepped out onto her balcony to water her plants and noticed a man going up the fire escape on Marie's building. He stopped at the window and looked like he was talking to someone, then he opened it and went inside."

"Did she see him leave?" I ask.

"No, but she said the lights went on inside the apartment and the next time she looked out there, they were still on. But then a while later, they were off again. And when we mentioned that to another neighbor, he said he did notice a man leave the building that night through the front door. He can't say for sure what time it was, but he didn't look out of place. His first thought was that he knew someone in the building."

"That sounds like probable cause to me," I say.

"It did to the judge, too."

"When do you get to go in?"

"Tomorrow."

"That's fantastic. Let me know how it goes," I say.

"Of course. And Emma?"

"Yes?"

"Try not to think too much about this. I know you're going to and that it's ridiculous for me to even say it because I know damn well you're not going to listen to me. But just try not to let your thoughts get carried away," he says.

"I don't know what you mean," I say innocently.

"Yes, you do," he says. "Let it be, babe. I know that's hard for you. I know it goes against everything in you. But sometimes you have to just take a step back. This is a tragedy. Young women who seem perfectly healthy aren't supposed to die so suddenly. But it does happen. And it did. It's harder because she meant a lot to Bellamy. Imagine how hard it is for her husband. This is his decision to make and his situation to work through. You can't make it happen differently because it's what you would do."

I know he's right. I hate that he's right. But I know he is.

"I love you," I say.

"I love you, too. Now don't let me hear from B that you've been up until the wee hours fretting on this."

"No promises."

CHAPTER TWELVE

I END THE CALL AND HEAD UP TO THE COUNTER FOR recommendations. It's nice to hear the girl behind the counter offer up a couple of the places I used to frequent when I was in school. Sometimes I forget how long ago that was. Before the watershed moment when I stepped out of the life I thought I was going to have and into the one that I'm leading now. Or some semblance of it, anyway.

Most of the time I don't feel old enough to be thinking about things like the next fifteen-year reunion I'll be invited to won't be for high school, but for college. Or that whoever is living in the dorm room where I used to study because I didn't live on campus is likely young enough to conceivably be my child.

Then there are other mornings when I get out of bed too fast and my joints sound like a bowl of puffed rice cereal with a fresh splash of milk and it all comes back to me.

But right now, I'm just happy to ignore the aches still lingering around in my body, pretend the scars I've picked up along the way aren't there, and order some of the wonderfully greasy food that used to fuel me through late-night studying and even later nights of not being able to sleep.

Insomnia and I go way back.

Accepting a handful of paper menus, I head back upstairs.

"What sounds good tonight? Thai, or something called Roly Poly that I haven't decided if it's a sandwich shop or a bakery specializing in Swiss rolls. You'd think having the menu would help me, but," I flip the little slip of pink and baby blue paper back and forth in my hand. "Nope. "

Bellamy doesn't answer and I look at her bed. She's still on top of the blankets and mostly sitting up, but fast asleep. I stop and toss the menus onto the dresser. I'll order something later. I go to her bed and pull the blanket from the end of it up so I can drape it over her. Turning off the lamp beside her doesn't do a lot of good, but it's at least a little bit dimmer in the room.

She's obviously exhausted. I doubt she's rested at all since finding out about Liza.

I take my phone and slip out of the sliding doors onto the small balcony. The chill wraps around me immediately and I go back in for a blanket to tuck around myself. Curling up on one of the two chairs sitting out on the suspended cement slab, I make a video call to Xavier.

It takes right up until my phone is about to give up and stop ringing for Xavier to answer, and when he does, I'm staring at his eyeball. This man can implant chips that allow him to track his friends. He has a house full of gadgets and machines and things I can only describe as booby traps. He walks around with more facts in his head than all the pie pieces in Trivial Pursuit put together. And yet he still can't figure out phone cameras.

He's getting better. Even if he does still peer into the webcam like he thinks I'm actually inside it.

"Move back a little, Xavier," I tell him. "I'm looking straight at your eye."

"Emma?"

"Just move back a little." He pushes back. He's still at an angle, but it's better. "There you are."

"Was I missing?"

"Not that I know of and please don't be. We've had enough of that recently," I say.

"I'll do my best."

It's a sincere statement coming from him.

"If I tell you some symptoms that a person has, can you tell me right off the top of your head what comes to mind?" I ask.

I know I could just plug the symptoms into good old reliable Dr. Google and get my answers that way, but I need the human element in this. Even if that human is Xavier. Come to think of it, he might be even more resourceful than Google itself when it comes to death. I want to see what kinds of conclusions he comes to and how quickly.

"Sure."

"Okay, so…"

"Wait."

"What?"

"Just anything that comes to mind?" he asks.

That seems like a particularly slippery slope to put myself on. He's going to need some set parameters.

"Diseases."

"On it. Proceed."

"Liza's husband Finn described her as feeling fine and then saying she felt sick. She was dizzy and disoriented, then got a headache and threw up. She was still throwing up and was having serious gastrointestinal upset before he called the ambulance."

"Dizzy, disoriented, headache, throwing up, diarrhea," he repeats over and over in a low voice. It's the worst mantra I've ever heard.

"Yes."

"Dead."

I swallow. "Yes. In just a matter of hours."

"Alright, well just coming right off the top of my head without putting a lot of thought into it, I'd go with cholera or Bubonic plague. I'll throw a flesh-eating bug in there just for some fun variety," he offers.

Well, I did ask him. This is on me.

"Cholera," I say.

"Mmmm-hmmmm."

"And Bubonic plague. As in the Black Death?"

"Mmmm-hmmmm. If you want to go with those titles, cholera used to be known as the Blue Death."

"Fantastic. So, the possibilities are two eradicated diseases," I say. "That's a good start."

"They weren't eradicated," Xavier corrects me. "A lot of people think that because they were so much more prevalent a long time ago, but both of those diseases still very much exist."

"They do?"

"Yes," he says. "There are about four million cases of cholera a year."

"Seriously?"

This is a total shock. I never would have considered either of those diseases as things that still happen, much less something that could be an actual risk of death.

"Yes." He pauses. "Well, I mean, worldwide. Not in the United States."

"How many in the U.S.?" I ask.

"Six."

"Six," I repeat. "How many cases of plague?"

"Bubonic?"

"Is there any other kind?" I ask with a frivolous flutter of my hand.

"Yes. Pneumatic. But that is characterized by more lung-based symptoms and you didn't say she was coughing or sneezing. If you want to get Biblical with it, the locust hordes that come every few years or so are thought of as a plague. There are some yearly deaths from that, but the symptoms of those kinds of deaths are things like cars smashed into trees and inhaled locusts."

"Bubonic," I say quickly, not knowing how much longer this portion of the conversation might continue and not really wanting to find out.

"Oh. More than cholera, actually."

"How many?"

"Seven."

I let out a sigh. "Perfect. So, fewer than ten people even get either of those diseases in this country each year. That's what I'm working with."

"Yes. And the flesh-eating bug. But that doesn't have a whole lot of cases, either. And the symptoms don't really line up all that well. Those little boogers can get into your bloodstream and wipe you out fast, though."

"I'm sure they can," I say.

"But if we're going by speed, I should also include meningitis."

My ears perk up a little. "Meningitis? That's a lot more common, isn't it?"

"About 2,600 cases a year in the U.S."

"Alright, well, not exactly common, but better than six."

"Or seven."

"Or seven," I agree.

"But that's just included by merit of the speed of death. The symptoms don't really line up," Xavier continues.

"So, we're back to bubonic plague and cholera," I say.

"Right off the top of my head," he says.

"Okay. Thank you, Xavier."

"You're welcome. That was fun. We should play that game more often. Want to give me another list of symptoms?"

"Maybe next time. Goodnight."

"Goodnight."

I hang up, but my phone rings almost instantly.

"Hello?"

"I just thought of another one. Ebola."

"Ebola?"

"Yes. It's not common, either. But it has the right symptoms and usually kills in a couple of days, but can kill much faster than that without correct treatment. But it's extremely, extremely infectious. All three of them are. Big outbreaks haven't happened in several years, you remember, but they have in others. It just takes one person getting infected through travel or infected marmoset meat and everybody is in trouble. Incidentally, that first person is referred to as Patient Zero—which I don't really understand, because they aren't zero. They are the one with the disease. The first one that was noticed. So, logically, that person should be Patient One. The rest of us who don't have it are actually zero. We're all Patient Zero."

That might be one of the most existential things I've ever heard Xavier say.

I'm choosing to ignore the marmoset meat.

"So, you would say those would be dangerous diseases if somebody were to have them and they weren't properly diagnosed?" I ask.

"Absolutely," he says. "Without a diagnosis, doctors wouldn't be able to take the proper precautions to prevent spread. Those diseases spread extremely quickly through person-to-person contact, contaminated food. Even respiratory droplets. It's extremely important to make sure anybody who has an infection with one of those gets an accurate diagnosis, so it doesn't become an outbreak."

Good enough for me.

CHAPTER THIRTEEN

The next day, I beg off when Bellamy makes plans to go see the rest of the group again. It feels like this is something she should do on her own. I know it's important to her that I'm here, and I'm happy to support her and help her through as much as I can. But they all have a shared history with Liza. They have memories of her and a connection that makes their grief something they should experience among themselves, at least for a time.

Bellamy agrees and thanks me with a tight hug before leaving the hotel. It's almost enough to make me feel a little bit guilty about what I have planned for the day. But I can't let myself feel that way. I can't let it stop me, anyway. The thing is, I know Sam's right. If Liza's husband is adamantly against the idea of an autopsy, that's his choice to make. There's a reason the law defers to the next of kin when making decisions like this. It isn't the place of anybody on the outside to make a choice about something so intimate and sensitive.

And for a married person, the next of kin is the husband or wife. That means that decision is Finn's and Finn's alone.

Only that's not enough for me. I can understand this is hard for him. The loss of a spouse is one of the most tragic and life-changing experiences anyone can have. But that could be exactly why Finn might not be thinking clearly. He doesn't want to make the situation any more difficult or show any disrespect to his late wife. But that means he likely isn't considering the repercussions for anyone else. He doesn't realize the impact his decision could make.

I don't want to cause him any more pain or difficulty, which is why I don't plan on talking to him. Maya came to pick Bellamy up so I would have access to the car during the day. I get in and head straight for the hospital.

"Are you family?" the hospital director, Luther Harris, asks later when I'm sitting in his office.

"No," I say.

He shakes his head as he crosses his office to the espresso machine set up on a marble counter against the wall. It always interests me when I see someone in the medical field doing something that seems to go against popular medical advice. Surgeons not wearing seatbelts. Nurses clustered around the ambulance bay of an emergency room smoking cigarettes. Hospital directors guzzling down high-octane coffee like water.

"Then I'm sorry, Ms..."

He looks at me with that expression of regret that comes over people who have too many things tumbling around in their heads for the name of someone they just met to stick.

Here I am. At a crossroads. There are two names I can give him, and I know very well they'll turn this conversation in different directions. Neither one is a lie, though. So... here I go.

"Griffin," I say.

He turns away from his machine with his tiny coffee cup in his hand and looks slightly confused as he blows over the hot beverage.

"Griffin," he muses, like he's trying it out to see if it actually is my name. "I'm sorry, I thought my secretary said something else."

I widen my eyes and nod like I'm just realizing what I said. "Oh. Yes. She probably said Johnson. That's my married name. It's still new."

"Well, congratulations," he says.

"Thank you. You know," I say, trying to make myself sound slightly playful, "it doesn't seem fair. You men don't have to get used to anything new after you get married. You are just Mister your whole life. But we have to get used to a whole new title and a new name. Now I'm Mrs. Johnson, but I'm still so used to saying Agent Griffin."

Harris pauses, his eyebrows raising slightly as he processes the title. There it is.

"Agent?" he asks.

I nod casually. "FBI."

"FBI?" he asks.

I know what's probably going through his mind right now. I'm not going to confirm it. I'm also not going to dissuade him. It's not technically unethical if I don't encourage him.

"Yep," I say. "The Bureau and I go way back. More than ten years now. Wow. I hadn't really thought about it that way. I've spent a whole decade of my life investigating."

He downs the rest of the espresso and sets the cup beside the machine. I can see the gears churning in his head as he comes back over to the desk. He sits down across from me and reaches for the phone in front of him.

"Dr. Kelsey, please," he says. He pauses. "Thank you." He waits another few seconds. "Sam, what can you tell me about Liza Fielding? Has her body been released yet?" He listens and nods. "Alright. Great. I'm going to be sending someone down to speak with you. She should be there in just a few minutes. Please answer her questions as thoroughly as possible."

He hangs up and I smile. "Sam. That's my husband's name."

He smiles in return. It's one of those smiles that doesn't light up his eyes, but there's at least some sincerity in it.

"This Sam is a Samantha. She was the head doctor for Mrs. Fielding's case. You can go down to her office and speak with her about it. She'll give you all the information she can."

"Thank you," I say, standing. "I appreciate it."

"You're welcome," he nods, already opening the files on his desk again to go back to work. "And congratulations again, Mrs. Griffin."

Close enough.

When I get to the office, a woman with sandy blonde hair now streaked with a bit of gray and kind wrinkles beside her eyes stands from behind the desk and walks toward me. She extends her hand.

"Dr. Samantha Kelsey," she introduces herself.

"Agent Emma Griffin," I tell her.

It feels like we're dueling titles. I've been in that position, throwing around acronyms and qualifications to see which rises to the top in the situation. Fortunately, this doesn't seem like one of those times when I need to flex to be heard. The warm-eyed doctor shakes my hand and smiles at me without any hesitation.

"Yes, Agent Griffin, come on in. What can I do for you?"

She closes the door behind me, and we walk over to a sitting area in the corner of the office rather than sitting across from each other at her desk.

"I came to ask about Liza Fielding," I say. "I'm guessing by the way the director spoke her body hasn't been released to her husband yet?"

"No, it hasn't," she confirms. "I chose to hold off on calling her husband to allow for the possibility of further testing."

She's being extremely careful with the words she chooses, but I don't need much elaboration. I've done my fair share of interacting with doctors over the years and I know by the way she put that she is waiting to see if Finn changes his mind about the autopsy or if the police get involved and request further clarification about her cause of death.

"I was hoping you would say that," I say. "Can you tell me your initial impressions about her cause of death?"

She hesitates, her expression reluctant. "I'm sorry, Agent Griffin, but I'm not able to release any information about a patient except to her family or by court order. Even deceased, she's protected by privacy laws."

"I'm familiar with the privacy laws," I say. "And I'm not asking you to divulge anything confidential. But cause of death is generally public knowledge. Cases like this end up in the media and details about her condition, her symptoms, and efforts to save the patients are discussed."

"But this case hasn't been discussed in the media," she counters.

"I understand that. I don't need any details about her health that don't have anything to do with this. I'm not asking for an outline of her treatments. I would just like to know what you observed and if you have any strong feelings about what might have happened to her." She hesitates again, looking clearly torn between wanting to answer my questions and maintaining her professional confidentiality.

"Look, I'll start it for you. I already know she started exhibiting symptoms just a few hours before she was brought into the hospital. She had dizziness and disorientation followed by nausea, vomiting, and diarrhea. Her death came quickly because you weren't able to immediately identify the cause of her distress, so you couldn't do anything to stop it."

Dr. Kelsey shifts in her seat and folds her hands over her knee where her leg is crossed over the other.

"Yes," she admits. "That is accurate."

I nod. "Alright. Now, I'm not a doctor. I don't know all the details or what those kinds of things do or don't indicate, but to me, that doesn't sound normal. Or at least common."

"They aren't," she says. "Liza Fielding was a healthy woman, by all accounts. Her husband presented her lifestyle as average or even a little above average in terms of taking care of herself. She hadn't suffered any extensive or serious illnesses in her past."

"So, in a situation like hers—not necessarily hers specifically—but one like hers," I prod, tilting my head forward slightly to indicate to her that I'm trying to give her an avenue to talk to me without blatantly breaking the law and her ethics. "You would consider it fairly unlikely that something was going on in her body that caused her death?"

"Right," she says. "Particularly for a woman, symptoms like dizziness, disorientation, nausea, vomiting, the types of symptoms a patient similar to Mrs. Fielding might have, could be indicative of a heart attack. But she did not have heart disease and her husband didn't report any acute stress or excessive exertion that might contribute to a fatal heart attack. I can't completely eliminate the possibility without an autopsy, but…"

"It doesn't seem likely," I complete the sentence.

She nods. "With the amount of time that passed between the onset of symptoms and death, the severity of the gastrointestinal symptoms, and the lack of reported chest pain, a heart attack is not the immediate assumption I would make."

"Even without authorization to do an autopsy, you can, in the course of normal medical treatment for any patient, collect samples for testing, correct?" I leave a slight pause, then tack on, "Just in general."

"Yes," she says. "That's normal practice."

"Blood?"

"Blood, urine. Any excretions."

I close my eyes briefly and let out a breath, not really believing I'm about to ask this question.

"Have you considered cholera or the Bubonic plague?" I ask.

Dr. Kelsey's mouth opens, then closes again. She seems to think about this question for a second, then shakes her head.

"I can't discuss specifics about a patient's health diagnoses, testing, or treatment," she says.

"I understand. Thank you for your time." I stand up but hesitate. "When is her body being released to her husband?"

"It should be by morning. It might be as early as this evening," she tells me.

I nod. "Alright. Until then, are you still able to collect samples?"

"I could," she acknowledges. "Things like hair and skin can still be done."

I nod. "Can I ask you to be discreet? Please don't discuss me being here, or any further samples you may or may not take, with anyone."

"Absolutely."

"Thank you for the information. Have a good day, Dr. Kelsey."

"You, too, Agent Griffin," she says.

I still feel a slight twinge of guilt as I walk out of the office, but I know I did the right thing. Finn's decision is an impulsive one made through emotion rather than completely thinking the situation through. It feels irresponsible to not find out what really happened to Liza, and that's something I can't do.

CHAPTER FOURTEEN

As I'm walking out of the hospital and across the parking lot, I hear my name. I know the voice immediately and my stomach sinks a little bit. I turn to see Bellamy coming toward me, a curious look on her face.

"What are you doing here, Emma?" she asks.

I wave my hand through the air to try to brush off the question casually.

"There were just a couple of questions I needed to ask the hospital director," I tell her.

"The hospital director?" she deadpans me. "Why would you talk to him?"

"Just some professional curiosity," I say. "Not a big deal."

"And you only spoke to him?" she asks.

She's asking me questions she already knows the answer to. I've known Bellamy long enough to know what she's thinking before she says it. And she knows me well enough to know I don't make it a habit of strolling into hospitals and having casual chats with hospital directors without there being a specific reason.

"Him and a doctor," I admit.

She rolls her eyes, giving up the curious act.

"I can't believe you did that, Emma. What is it about people's boundaries and privacy you just don't understand?"

"Wow," I say. "That's a little harsh."

"What's a little harsh is a good friend of mine is standing over there across the parking lot right now getting ready to go into a hospital, where his dead wife's body is lying in the morgue. He's coming here to sign over paperwork to donate her organs and authorize the release of her body to the funeral home so she can be cremated. That's harsh," she hisses.

"He's having her cremated?" I ask.

"Yes," she says. "And that's none of your business, either. None of this is."

"You brought me here, Bellamy."

"Don't put this on me. I brought you here because you're my best friend and I thought you would be supportive and make me feel better while I grieve over the very sudden death of a friend I've had for more than fifteen years. Not so that you could turn her death into a source of entertainment for yourself," she says.

"That's not what I'm doing, Bellamy," I protest. "You said it yourself. A very sudden death. This was by all rights a healthy woman who took care of herself. Maybe nothing extreme or over-the-top, but she was healthy. A good weight. No chronic health problems, right?"

"Why does that matter, Emma? She's dead."

"Exactly. Everything was fine and then her body just suddenly decided to give out?"

"It happens," she says.

"Sometimes, yes. Sometimes the heart is a bitch in ways that don't involve little candies with messages written on them or sappy songs that make you want to fling yourself off a bridge. A heart attack is not impossible, but it also isn't the first thing that comes to mind. It doesn't fit. Which means something else killed her. Diseases and infections that kill that quickly are dangerous, Bellamy. And just pushing that aside because it's too hard to think about is irresponsible," I say.

She shakes her head. "You're unbelievable sometimes. You can't just accept that things happen. That sometimes having all the little details doesn't help. It doesn't change anything. Liza is still dead. Finn is a widower. He's not even forty years old yet and he is a widower. Do you know all the plans they had? Things they were going to do together?"

"No," I admit.

"They were going to go to Europe next year. He was setting it up as a surprise for her to celebrate their anniversary. He's been planning it for years. She had just started training to run her first half-marathon in the spring. Last week she posted pictures of all the Thanksgiving baking dishes and serving pieces she had gotten out of the attic to clean and get ready for the holiday.

"She loved Thanksgiving. It was her favorite time of year, and she would spend weeks thinking about her menu and days cooking with her family. I haven't been to one of her Thanksgivings since college. And you know why? Because I've always been with you. Now, Finn is facing those dishes sitting out on the counters and in the dining room. He says he hasn't even been able to bring himself to move them because she put them there. He still can't wrap his head around the idea that she won't be making Thanksgiving dinner.

"He did everything he could to save her. He tried to get her help. But he couldn't. He didn't realize anything was seriously wrong with her. She just felt a little bit sick, like all of us do every now and then. When you have a headache and your stomach starts to feel sick, the first thing that comes to mind isn't that you're going to be dead within a few hours. But he had to watch his wife die after waking up with her perfectly healthy. Do you think going through all the invasive efforts of finding out exactly what it was is going to make any difference to him?

Is it going to change that she's not there anymore? That all those plans aren't going to happen?"

"Knowing why something happened can help with the grief," I fire back.

"You aren't trying to find out why it happened, you're trying to find out how. They aren't the same thing. And in this, there is no why. And that's the reason Finn doesn't want to make the situation more painful for himself by going through all that. It's as much as he can do to deal with the grief and keep putting one foot in front of the other. It's been less than three days."

"I just don't understand how he could not want to know," I say.

"That's the thing, Emma. You don't need to understand. It's not up to you. All that matters is what's right for Finn, and he's decided. You need to back off."

She turns away and I take a step toward her. "Bellamy..."

"No," she says, shaking her head as she turns back to me. "Emma, back off. I love you, but I can't back you up on this. And I can't deal with it right now. I need to go be with Finn and the others. I'll meet you at the hotel in a few hours so we can leave. I'm ready to go home."

I watch her walk away, her words heavy in the pit of my chest.

I don't go directly back to the hotel. Instead, I drive around the city that I used to call home. It's not the same as it was then, of course. Years change things. Everything. Even a place this historic and seemingly set in its ways. But there are still plenty of things that are just as they were, and every one I see brings back memories of that time.

The memories shift over to thoughts of the upcoming Thanksgiving holiday. Like Liza, this has always been my favorite time of year. I love decorating the house and preparing the meal. Even when the smells and tastes make me ache for my mother and my grandparents, it's worth the joy of being with those closest to me and taking some time to savor moments of gratitude.

I have to admit the holiday is going to be a little bit different this year. Whether I want to think about him this way or not, the reality is

Jonah is my family. He's my uncle, my father's identical twin brother. In any other circumstances, in any other life, he would have a place at my Thanksgiving table.

Of course, if we were in those other circumstances, in that other life, my mother would be at that table as well. Dean wouldn't. Xavier wouldn't.

This puts me in the strange position of thinking about alternate versions of my life and all the ways it would change what I know. For the better and for the worst. I don't plan on changing anything about Thanksgiving this year. Not intentionally, anyway. It's not like I can invite Jonah to come to dinner. He's not about to come calling with a bottle of wine in hand, ready to sit down for turkey and mashed potatoes. I can't see myself ever passing him the peas without a very strong side of handcuffs.

But thinking about him being out in the world makes me wonder about the holidays when I was really little. I know now that he was fully cast out of my family's lives when I was seven years old. That's when he tried to take me, and the clash ended with my family thinking he was dead. My parents cut him out before I was even born. But I honestly don't know if that means they didn't see each other at all or how many holidays they might have spent together before I came along.

Jonah talks about always being in love with my mother. I know that they were close at least at one point. I still have the picture of them, a picture I always thought was her with my father. They are standing close together, smiling at the camera.

What were those holidays like? What was his favorite food? Did my grandmother used to smack him on the hand because he would reach for a yeast roll before the blessing? Did he toss more of those rolls across the table to his brother like they might have when they were kids? Was he a pumpkin pie person or a sweet potato pie person? Maybe he preferred pecan or even chocolate?

Did he ever celebrate Thanksgiving with Leviathan?

CHAPTER FIFTEEN

When I get back to the hotel and toss my phone onto the dresser along with the keycard, I notice it's blinking to let me know I have notifications. I check it and realize I never turned the ringer off silent that morning and I've missed several calls from Sam.

I sit down at the end of the bed holding the phone to my ear with my shoulder while I take off my shoes.

"Hey, babe," I say when he answers. "Sorry I missed your calls. I turned the sound off the phone to try to get some sleep last night and I forgot to turn it off this morning before I headed out. Is everything alright?"

"I got to go into Marie's apartment today," he tells me.

"Oh, that's right," I say. "The search warrant went through. How did it go?"

"She wasn't in there," he says. "I guess that kind of goes without saying. It was wishful thinking that we might be able to just walk into her apartment and find her sitting there, having decided she was done with the world and needed some time to herself."

"That doesn't sound like Marie," I point out.

"No, it doesn't," he sighs. "But neither does any of this. But at least we also didn't find her body."

"That is a good thing," I note. "So, I guess it was a dead end? The guy they saw going into her apartment was probably just a run-of-the-mill burglar?"

"I don't know if I would go that far," Sam says. "I still don't know who the man that the neighbor saw going into the apartment was, or why he was there, but the search didn't come up completely empty."

"What did you find?" I ask, tossing myself back to recline on the pillows.

"A couple of notes with addresses and comments that kind of looked like her handwriting, but I can't be completely positive. We're looking into those, trying to find out what the addresses are and what the comments might mean. They were just some words like 'blue', 'old', 'repeat'. Things that really don't string together into an entire thought. Then there was a note that was obviously written in someone else's handwriting. It looks like a list, but it's pretty unintelligible."

"That doesn't sound like much," I say, not wanting to be discouraging, but feeling disappointed for Sam. I know he was really depending on the search coming up with something useful in finding his cousin—or at least getting closer to knowing what happened to her.

"Well, that's just where things get interesting," he says.

"You aren't saying that in that fun way that means things are about to get exciting or playful," I say.

"Because they aren't," Sam admits. "But we did find a couple of other things. Kind of hidden away in her bedroom we found a cell phone I don't recognize, and neither did my aunt when I showed her a picture of it. It's an old-style flip phone."

"A flip phone?" I ask.

"Yeah," he confirms. "I haven't seen anybody over the age of twelve and under the age of sixty-five use one of those in like a decade. But there it was. We were able to get some contacts off of it and we're going to look into them to see if we can find out anything. There weren't too many numbers in it, not like she was using it for contacting her friends and family."

"Was it a burner?"

"Possibly," he says. "Or just a phone that she used to get in touch with people she didn't want other people to know about."

"I think that's what a burner is, Sam," I point out.

He lets out a sigh and I can almost see him rubbing his eyes with his fingertips. It means he's exhausted and a tension headache is starting to form in the back of his head. When they happen, he says it feels like rubber bands are attached to the backs of his eyeballs and somebody is slowly turning a gear that pulls them tighter and tighter.

"I know," he says. "I'm just hoping it's actually registered to her. That makes it less suspicious and seem less like all of this has been going on right in front of the family and we didn't know about it."

"What do you mean?" I ask. "All of what going on?"

"We found drugs," he says.

I'm surprised by the revelation. I don't know Marie all that well, but I've never gotten any indication she had anything to do with drugs, or even that she was carrying around a secret like that. Not that it's always immediately obvious when someone has a problem with a substance or has been struggling with addiction. That's often the most dangerous part of that type of situation. It goes unnoticed because the person learns how to hide it and keep going with their lives until it just can't be sustained anymore.

Family and friends can't help if they don't know what's wrong. They just watch while their loved one crashes and burns seemingly out of nowhere.

But even knowing that, it's shocking and a little confusing to think about Marie being deeply involved in drugs. I understand what Sam means by hoping the phone is registered and not a hidden burner. If it's registered, at least she's still up on the surface a little bit. She hasn't sunk all the way down into the depths of creating a dense, complex web to support her hidden activities out of the eyes of those closest to her.

"A lot?" I ask carefully. "Enough just for her personal use, or does it look like she might have been dealing?"

"I don't know," Sam says. "What we found doesn't look like enough to sustain dealing. It's more than I would think one person would have for regular recreational use, but that could mean that she is a heavy user or just wanted to stock up. But we also found some bags and a couple of surfaces with residue."

"Which could mean that she had a considerable amount more at her apartment and it was sold. Or it was used."

"Right."

"I'm sorry, babe," I say. "Is there anything I can do?"

"Not right now," he says. "The department is sending in the CSU to do a more thorough investigation of the whole apartment now that a search confirmed criminal activity. And hopefully, we'll be able to find whoever that man was."

"The neighbor wasn't able to give you a good description?" I ask.

"No. Neither person who said they saw a man going into or out of her apartment could say anything more than it was a man. Extremely generic. Medium height. Medium build. They couldn't see hair color or features because it was cold that night and he had a hat on and his collar pulled up. That didn't strike them as strange, and they didn't think they needed to pay attention and catch any other details about him."

"How about security cameras?" I ask. "Does her building have one?"

"It doesn't," Sam says. "But the laundromat around the corner does. It's positioned at an angle from her building, so even if the camera was functioning that night, it wouldn't have gotten a clear image of anybody near it. But it could have caught something. Right now, we're just hoping for anything. Now that it's actually considered a case, a detective has taken over. They requested the footage from the owner, but we haven't heard back yet."

I know it's driving him insane that he is having to rely on other people to handle this investigation. While he keeps saying "we" and including himself when he mentions the investigation or the police department, the truth is he isn't actually a part of it. He's being given professional courtesy by the department because he is a sheriff, but at any point, they could take the investigation in a completely different direction than he would want it to go and he won't be able to say anything about it.

He can't control what they look into or how they interpret evidence. He can't make any arrests. He can only hope they will keep him informed and continue to allow him to participate.

"Let me know if you think of anything I could look into for you," I tell him. "I'm sorry I can't be there with you."

"I know. I am too. But you're doing what you need to do right now. How is it going there, by the way? How is Bellamy holding up?" he asks.

"She's not great," I admit. I feel the guilt come back a little stronger. "She's upset with me."

"Upset with you?" he asks. "Why would she be upset with you?"

"Because I might have gone to the hospital to talk to the doctor about Liza Fielding's death."

"Emma! What were you thinking?" he gasps. "We already talked about this and you agreed you needed to stay out of it."

"I know," I sigh, feeling more than a little embarrassed about it. "I know I did. But don't you think it's important to find out what happened to her? The doctor obviously couldn't tell me everything, but she did make sure I knew Liza was a healthy woman and the onset of her symptoms was strange. It could have been a heart attack, but she doesn't think so, and without an autopsy, she can't know for sure."

"So, you thought you'd go in there and demand an autopsy?" he asks.

"No," I reply. Maybe telling him what I did wasn't the best choice at this particular moment. "I just asked some questions and found out if she had taken any particular samples before the body went to the morgue."

The door to the room opens right as I'm saying the sentence and I can't stop the words no matter how much I want to push them back into my mouth. Bellamy rolls her eyes and slams the door behind her.

"What was that?" Sam asks.

"Bellamy just back to the room," I say.

"Have fun with that," he says. "Maybe next time you'll actually stay out of it when you know you should."

"It could be cholera," I attempt.

"Emma."

"I'll talk to you later."

Bellamy is shoving her clothes into her suitcase when I end the call and set the phone down beside me, sitting up from the pillows.

"I guess you decided you hadn't invaded Finn and Liza's privacy enough, so you had to get a few more people involved?" she grumbles.

I understand she's frustrated and angry with me, and I can accept that. She's going through a lot right now. But she's pushing it.

"That was Sam," I say. "I think I'm allowed to speak to my husband. Or is that out of line, too?"

She glares at me. "Are you seriously going to try to act like you have a place being indignant right now?"

"Look, B, I know you don't like what I did."

"But that doesn't matter, does it?" she asks. "You wanted to do it and you thought it was the right thing to do, so you went ahead and did it without thinking about anyone else."

I stare at her, stunned into temporary silence. "What in the living hell is this? Did you and Eric get together with everybody and have a conference about how much I piss all of you off? Is this a really drawn-out intervention I should be prepared for? Who's next? Are you going to send Dean in to talk about me stepping over his dead mother and not realizing it? Or Xavier to show off the scars around his neck and how the guy who actually killed Andrew might get off because I haven't been able to find enough evidence to prove he did it?"

"Emma," she says, rolling her eyes.

"No, no, who next? Sam? Or my father? Because both of them have plenty to say. Is there a specific timetable for these, or are you just kind of tossing them in whenever it feels like it would be fun for you?" I ask.

"I think you're overreacting," Bellamy says.

"Just like you are about Liza."

We stare at each other for a long beat.

"It wasn't your place, Emma."

"All I did was ask some questions. That's it. I don't understand what's so wrong about that," I protest.

Bellamy sags under the question, looking at me in a way I can only imagine Xavier sees all the time. A look that says there's something I should understand and she can't grasp why I don't. Like she's expecting me to be able to climb through a brick wall to her.

"Emma, sometimes you have to stop being an FBI agent and just be a person. You don't have to go into every situation thinking and analyzing. Sometimes, you just need to feel. This is one of those situations. You don't need to know the inner workings of everything. Explanations don't always offer good. Sometimes they just hurt more. Finn is already grieving. He probably feels like he did something wrong or that he didn't do enough to protect her from whatever infection killed her.

Do you really think it's going to make a difference to him to find out what that infection was? I know for some people finding out every detail is comforting. It brings closure. They want to know exactly what happened and how, but that's not everybody. Maybe he doesn't want to start thinking about where she picked it up and if it was something he did. If she got it from food that he bought or a place he brought her. Or if he somehow got her sick."

"But that's my whole point," I counter. "If any of those things happened to her, they could happen to someone else. Someone else could eat the food that's contaminated. Someone else could touch the surface and pick up the bug. Someone else could contract the infection. By not finding out, he could cause a public health crisis."

"Then that's for the authorities to find out, when or if they find the cause," she presses. "Not for you."

"I'm an FBI agent, B. It's my job. I take this very seriously."

"I know, and that's why I love you, but please, Emma…" she takes a deep, frustrated breath. "It's not your job to burst in and solve other people's problems. It's not your job to go behind my back and meddle in people's personal affairs. I asked you to come because I needed your support. As a friend. Not as an agent. Not because I wanted your help in solving the case. But because I thought you would understand."

I open my mouth to reply, but she holds up a hand to stop me. "No, sorry. I'm not done. You're very lucky that I caught you before Finn and the others saw you. I love you to death, Emma, but your bedside manner is… not the greatest. I don't even want to know what kind of hell would have erupted if Finn or the others found out what you did back there. What you might have thought would have been trying to bring closure, he would have thought was a level of personal disrespect to his dead wife. You're very strong in your convictions, and I've always admired that about you. But just because they're your convictions doesn't mean you have the right to trample over others to get what you want. You don't get to barge in on people's lives like this."

I feel a little slapped by the words, but I don't say anything. She's right.

Bellamy sighs and finishes packing. "Finn has never believed in autopsies, Emma. Never. He talked about it in college during one of his classes and then when his grandmother died and his grandfather requested one. It's not your way. It might not be my way. But it's his way and in this situation, that's all that really matters. I don't think Liza's death is going to cause the next pandemic. You trying to force an autopsy isn't going to do anything but hurt Finn and make my friends angry."

"I didn't try to force an autopsy. You know as well as I do that I can't do that. All I did was ask about the samples the doctor took and when the body was going to be released," I finally say.

"And that's more than enough," she says. "Can I please just ask that you not do this anymore?"

I take a deep breath. "Okay. I'm sorry."

CHAPTER SIXTEEN

The drive back from Alexandria was the longest stretch of time Bellamy and I have ever gone without speaking to each other and I'm still thinking about it the next day as I sit on the floor in the living room at Dean and Xavier's house. I'm trying to go over everything I know about Miley, Serena, and the Emperor, trying to find more connections or details I might have missed, but I'm struggling to focus.

"The answer is twenty-two," Xavier announces as he comes into the room.

I look up at him with confusion. "The answer to what?"

"Whatever you're thinking so hard about. I figure 22 is a really good number. It is a pair of twos which is the base of all even numbers, so an even number of even numbers, which means nobody gets left behind, not even the source of that which eliminates the need for extraneous items in a group that may be at risk of being left behind. It's a good answer. And if it's wrong, then at least you've answered the question.

Once you answer a question and get it wrong that means you can go back and fix it."

"I like the way you think, Xavier."

He shrugs, dropping down into the chair beside me and turning so his leg drapes over the arm and his head rests against the large wing of the back.

"It's just logic," he says.

"If you say so," I chuckle.

I look back down at the documents in front of me.

"Still trying to figure out how Salvador didn't know the woman he called Miley wasn't actually her?" he asks.

"Yep. And also trying to find more of his arenas. Something Jonah said the last time I talked to him really made me think about how Salvador worked as a killer. He was meticulous in his planning. He knew exactly what he wanted and how he wanted it. There was nothing arbitrary or sudden or spontaneous about anything that he did. Which means there are definitely other killing grounds somewhere. We just have to find them."

"Look for the helpers," Xavier offers. "That's what Mister Rogers always used to tell us."

I look over at him. "You are talking about on TV, right? You didn't live in Mister Rogers' Neighborhood and like hang out with Daniel Tiger or anything?"

"On TV," he clarifies as if he's confirming a completely logical possibility. "But he did. He always said look for the helpers. It's what his mama taught him. If something was going wrong, look for the helpers."

I nod, not really knowing what to do with that piece of advice. That's not all that unusual. I'm under the belief that my brain has manufactured a new area within it dedicated solely to containing and attempting to unravel the things Xavier says. Some of them take longer than others. I'm thinking this might be one of those.

After a few seconds, I look over at him.

"Do I think about myself over other people?" I ask.

He looks down at the papers spread across the floor in front of me.

"Is that in there somewhere as a prerequisite? Because he's dead. He's not going to come after you no matter how many of the things on his checklist you fit," Xavier frowns.

"No. I just mean in general," I say.

"Oh." He thinks only for a fraction of a second. "Yes."

"I think I like 22 as an answer better," I mutter, turning my attention back to the papers.

"Why?"

I look back at him incredulously.

"Seriously? You're now the second person today who's informed me I'm selfish and self-centered and don't think about anybody else when I make decisions. The second person who is really important to me, by the way. If it had just been anybody else, somebody I didn't know or didn't care about, it wouldn't be such a big deal. But it was you and Bellamy," I sigh.

"Well, yeah. But it's not always a bad thing," Xavier says. "You're not selfish or self-centered. But you have a very strict, defined way of viewing the world. You think about yourself and what you feel in your gut more than you think about other people's opinions or if it might upset them. That's what makes you such a great agent. It also makes it hard for you to consider things from other people's viewpoints. You're not afraid to throw your elbows around or push people out of your way when you've got a hunch about something. And usually, you're right."

"Usually?"

Xavier nods. "Usually. But not always. Sometimes your hunch is absolutely correct and everyone else is ten steps behind you. But sometimes you're lost, wandering out there in the field."

"Wow," I comment. "You really think that?"

Xavier tilts his head as if not sure why I even asked. "Of course I do. I wouldn't have said it otherwise. Because you know you're the one who has to make the decision to do something not convenient or comfortable. So other people's opinions are simply not relevant. I think that's why you and I get along so well. Not everybody can do that."

"Not everybody can be selfish?" I ask with an edge of sarcasm.

"Not everybody can make the hard decisions that you do. Not everybody can care deeply and not at all at the same time. In every kingdom, there are the knights and there is the Queen. It just so happens you are both."

"Thank you, Xavier. I think?"

"Always." He swings his legs around and slides down onto the floor to sit beside me. "Did this have something to do with the Ebola patient?"

"It wasn't Ebola," I say. "But, yes."

"What was it?" he asks.

"They don't know."

"Then it could have been Ebola."

"That's true. It could have. But we don't know because the widower of the woman who died wouldn't give permission for an autopsy."

"Why not?" Xavier asks.

"That is a really fantastic question," I tell him. "And it really bothers me that it even has to be asked. Because what if this is some sort of infectious outbreak? He could be putting other people at risk."

"Do you really think that?" Xavier asks.

"What do you mean?" I ask.

"Do you really think that she could have died from some sort of illness and that it's putting a lot of people at risk? Or is it that you just can't stand the idea of not knowing what ended somebody's life?" he asks.

He can see right through me. He's always been able to. I don't even know why I try.

"Both," I admit. "I don't think it's fair for anybody to be taken off this Earth without their story being told, and a big part of anybody's story is the end of it. She had an entire life ahead of her, so why is it over? Even if it is something as simple as she got an infection, don't you think that her husband would want to know that?"

"Why does this bother you so much?" he asks.

"I don't know," I say. "It just feels like it can't possibly be as simple as everybody wants to think it is. And if it is that simple, why hide from it? I just don't like the possibility of questions being asked that can't ever be answered. And without the autopsy, that's what will happen. So, I made the decision to go into the hospital and talk to the doctor about her body."

"Emma."

"I didn't demand an autopsy," I raise my hands in protest at his warning. "I didn't pick up a scalpel and do it for her. I just asked about biological samples that could be used to uncover the cause of death."

"This is exactly what I mean. You made that decision because, thinking of yourself, it was the right thing to do. You didn't care about how that would affect anyone else."

That sends another lance of embarrassment through me. "Tell me about it. B nearly read me the riot act in the hotel that night."

Something flickers in the back of my mind, like a sparkle of color.

"Technically speaking, I can't tell you about it, because I wasn't..." he trails off. "What just happened? You just got that look in your eyes."

"Bellamy said that Finn has always been against autopsies. He thinks that they're disrespectful and that they don't really help anything because finding out how someone died doesn't do any good," I explain.

"That's not true," Xavier says.

"No, it's not. But that's not all. He said he doesn't want to disrespect her body. He doesn't like the idea of anyone cutting her open and taking parts of her out," I say.

He shrugs slightly. "I suppose I can understand that. I mean, if they aren't using them, why does it really matter? It's kind of fun to think about. Like an unboxing video. Just squishy. And no potential for anything limited edition, because they're all pretty much the same once you get past the packaging."

"Exactly. She isn't using them. So, someone else was going to," I nod. "When I was talking to the doctor, I asked when the body was going to be released to the funeral home. She said she was waiting on authorization and for Liza's organs to be harvested for donation. A husband who thinks that an autopsy is disrespecting his wife's body is fine with harvesting her for donation? And then cremating her? That doesn't fit together.

"And even if he could separate it, even if he could say that he didn't believe in autopsies, but he thinks organ donation is acceptable because it can help someone else, they wouldn't be able to do that. They can't just arbitrarily take someone's organs out and put them in someone else without knowing if they are healthy and functioning. With an unknown cause of death, that would be too big of a risk. They would have to do all the tests and everything to find out if the organs were safe for use."

I take Xavier by his cheeks and look him right in the eye.

"I might have to be the Queen and a knight, but you. You are Merlin."

I rush back to my room where my computer is sitting and open it. Searching for the hospital, I scroll through the faculty information until I find Dr. Kelsey. I call her office and leave a message for her to video call me as soon as possible.

It doesn't take long for her to call me back. Her eyebrows are already pulled together with curiosity and perhaps a little confusion when her face fills the screen.

"Agent Griffin?" she says by way of greeting.

"Emma," I say. "Thank you for calling me back."

"No problem," she says. "I don't have a lot of time, but what can I do for you?"

"I've been thinking about Liza Fielding," I say.

"I told you everything that I can," she says.

"I know," I acknowledge. "But I was thinking about how generous it was for her husband to agree to her organ donation."

Her eyes widen just slightly. I only notice because I'm looking for a reaction.

"Yes," she confirms. "I'm always humbled by people who are willing to take a moment in their time of grief to consider the lifesaving gift of donating their loved one's organs."

"I find it especially impressive considering her husband's feelings on autopsy," I remark. "Tell me, doctor, how did you find recipients willing to accept organs from a donor with completely unknown health and cause of death?"

A slight smile curls at her lips. She knows I figured her out.

"When a death like that happens, I always want to know what happened. Even if there is an extremely simple explanation, I want to know it," she says.

"I feel the exact same way," I say.

"I want you to understand something. I didn't steal her organs. I spoke to her husband myself and he expressed his feelings on having his wife autopsied. He said he couldn't stand the idea of somebody cutting her open just to find out that she was sick or had an infection. They didn't have children, so there was no genetic component. But he did specifically say that if it seemed like there could be a suspicious cause of death, potentially foul play, behind the death of someone he loved, he would agree to an autopsy," she says.

"Did you explain to him that her death was suspicious?" I ask.

"Yes," she nods. "But because there were no outward signs of an attack or any indication that something happened to her, in fact, it looks very much like she just fell sick and died, he wouldn't agree to it."

"But you think there could be something else."

"I don't know if there is. As I said, it could just be an infection.

An illness she's had for a while that we just didn't know about. There is any number of explanations, but because there are any number of explanations, it's absolutely necessary to cover all our bases when it comes to finding out the truth. I could be brought up on ethics charges for it."

"Not if nobody knows," I say. "Organs are harvested for donation and never given to a recipient all the time, are they?"

"Yes," she says. "I put in a record that they were harvested and have them stored. Because they can't be used for a recipient, it doesn't matter if they are preserved to the extent of being functional again. We just need the tissues."

"Have you already sent them for toxicology?"

"Yes. It might take a couple weeks, especially since it's not a high-profile case. But it's out there."

"You are incredible," I say. "Thank you for doing that."

"You don't remember me, do you?" she asks.

I wasn't expecting that.

"Should I?" I ask.

Another hint of a smile comes to her lips, but this one is sadder and more nostalgic than amused. She nods just slightly.

"It's alright. It was a long time ago and you had a lot going on at the time. I don't expect you to remember," she says.

"What do you mean?" I ask.

"I worked at the hospital in DC when Greg Bailey was first found. I helped take care of him," she explains. "I didn't want to say anything to you when I saw you yesterday. I figured you wouldn't remember, and I didn't want to cause more disruption in what you were already going through. But I just felt like you should know I understand why you think something is off."

"Thank you," I tell her. "Both for that and for taking care of him. I'm sorry I don't remember meeting you."

"No," she says. "Please, don't apologize. I know there was so much going on and you couldn't be expected it to take in everything around you."

It's another reminder of my effect on others that I hadn't considered before. Yet more proof that my actions flow out like ripples, even if I'm not aware of them.

"Thank you," I repeat. I don't really know what to say. "How did you end up at a different hospital?"

"It might not shock you to hear I started questioning things after that incident," she says. "When Mr. Creagan got wind of it, he made sure there was no pressure put on at the hospital administration and I was transferred out."

"I'm sorry that happened to you. But I'm glad you were here."

"So am I."

"I really hope it's for nothing," I say.

"So do I."

CHAPTER SEVENTEEN

Two days later, I'm back at Miley Stanford's house. Xavier's words are still bouncing around in my head. Find the helpers. Look for the helpers. I'm not entirely sure what he meant by them, but they've started to take root a little bit. Maybe not in the way he intended, and maybe not in any way that will actually amount to anything, but I have to have something to go on.

I park in front of the house and stare at it for a few seconds. I'm not really waiting for anything. Or maybe I am. That house has seen a lot. Likely far more than I have even begun to realize. Miley has been missing for well over a year. Her neighbors report to not have realized it because there was someone else living in the house the whole time who looked just like her. I know that person to be Serena, but it still doesn't make any sense. I still don't understand why she ended up there, why Jonah chose this house in this neighborhood to hide a refugee from a crime family who he won in a poker game and paid for with a murder.

The house is owned by Miley's parents, who live overseas. Even when we contacted them to inform them that their daughter had died, or so we thought, they seemed completely unconcerned about it. They didn't even come home to follow up with authorities. It's another strange mystery lurking in the shadows of this house.

I get out of my car and pull my jacket around myself to ward off the November chill. It feels colder here than it does in Sherwood. I don't know if that's just my imagination or some sort of strange Norman Rockwell-esque hometown magic situation, but it feels distinctly colder in this neighborhood even though we are only a couple of hours apart, and geographically speaking, Sherwood should have a colder climate.

I'm stalling. I'm standing right outside my car, contemplating the weather so that I don't have to walk up to the door. It's not the door to the neat, well-cared-for little house in front of me I'm hesitating going to. Instead, it's the neighbor next door I need to speak with. I don't want to. I have talked to her before and she's less than pleasant. But I really don't care about that. Life in the FBI doesn't exactly surround you with unicorns and butterflies all the time. I tend to be treated with spite and resistance far more often than I am kindness, so I'm used to it.

It's what I'm asking her that gives me pause. As much as I want to hear what she has to say, I also don't. It means opening more doors to delve deeper into Jonah's life and everything he's done that I don't even know about. I already know enough to last me a lifetime. A few lifetimes. But it seems there's always a need to go deeper. Just when I think I have scraped away enough layers and exposed enough of the slimy, cold, beating mass that is where Jonah's heart should be, I realize there's more to find out. There are more secrets I have to learn.

The day I refuse to do anymore, when I give up and walk away, is the day I'd tell all of his victims I don't care what he did to them. It's the day I would make myself just another way the world went dark on them. That's not something I can bring myself to do. I won't say there aren't moments when I haven't tried. I've come to what I thought was my breaking point more times than I care to think about.

But as far as he pushes me, as much as he tries to break me, I won't let him. I keep going. And I will keep going as long as I can.

And that includes today.

The neighbor standing behind the door is just about as happy to see me as she was the first time I showed up at her door. She peers at me through the tiniest crack possible in the door, making sure I can see that the slide lock is still in place, the chain stretched across her face as she looks at me.

"Hi," I say. "I'm Agent Griffin, I've spoken with you before."

"I know," she says. "I'm not so old that I can't remember something that happened a couple of weeks ago."

Thank you for the segue.

"I know. And that's actually what I was hoping to talk to you about."

I'm waiting for her to invite me in out of the cold, but she doesn't. She looks me up and down and gives a single, defiant nod.

"Go ahead," she says.

"The last time we spoke, we talked about the woman who lived next door," I say.

We've been extremely careful about what we have released to the media, not wanting to expose too many of the details of the case and potentially compromise any information we might get. That means we haven't spoken about the fact that the body found was a woman masquerading as someone else. I have to tread lightly, not feeding the neighbor any information or guiding her in anything she might say.

"Yes," she nods.

"You said you didn't know much about her because your neighborhood is very private," I continue. "That you don't interact with each other or pay much attention to what the others are doing."

"That's right."

"But you watched her," I say. "I know you did."

"I didn't do anything of the kind," she replies.

"Yes, you did. You told me she had red hair and she looked like that cartoon woman from the movie. You were talking about Jessica Rabbit, weren't you? Your neighbor owned a red sparkly dress that looked very much like the one that character wore. Did you make that comparison because you watched her and saw her in that dress?" I ask.

She has a tense expression like she's trying to come up with some sort of explanation, then finally relents.

"Fine, I watched her sometimes. Not doing anything… untoward, mind you. Just going about her life. I only noticed her because she had the most outlandish wardrobe and wigs to go with it. She always seemed to be showing up in different kinds of clothes or going out with different hair and different makeup. It was like she was an actress," she says.

This makes absolute sense to me. I happen to know it's because she did pretend to be various different kinds of people. She changed her own identity to infiltrate other people's lives and manipulate them into becoming exactly what Salvador asked for. Serena was his goddess. He would pray to her for a specific type of victim, and she would provide.

"Is there anything else you know about her? Anything else at all that you could tell me? It doesn't have to be from any time recently. In fact, maybe something from a while ago would be useful. Something from years back, maybe? When she might have looked even more different than she does now?"

I know I am leading a bit, but I bite my tongue, keeping myself from giving away any more information. I know this woman knows more. It's just a matter of finding out how to get it from her.

"A long while back, she did seem different," the neighbor admits after a moment of thought.

"All right," I say. "How so? What was different about her?"

"She still went out all the time. But she didn't wear all the outlandish outfits. She just wore expensive clothes and drove an expensive car. She never once looked up and smiled. Maybe that's the big difference. I think the whole reason she came over to use my phone was because I waved at her once."

"You waved at her?" I ask.

"Yes," she says. "It had been a little while since I've even noticed somebody moving around in the house and I hadn't seen her car in several days. It showed back up at the house and when she got out, she looked right over at me. I was sitting on the porch and instead of her just grabbing her things out of the back seat and stomping up the sidewalk like she always did, she paused for a second and looked over and waved."

"Do you remember anything about what she looked like that day? Maybe what she was wearing? Or what color her hair was?" I ask.

"Dark hair," she says. "Not that that gives you much to go on considering it seems everybody's days has dark hair. I swear, it used to be blond, but now everywhere I look there are people dyeing their hair dark. Makes them look like they dunked their heads in tar. You haven't thought about doing that, have you?"

"No," I tell her, shaking my head. "I've never dyed my hair."

"Good. You keep that blond right like it is. You'll age just fine."

Exactly what I want to hear.

"So, you say she never looked over at you or smiled or waved or anything before that? Would you characterize her as rude?" I ask.

"Not rude," she says. "Just distracted, maybe. Like there's always something else she was supposed to be doing. Then later she was still busy all the time, but oh, I don't know, there was just something different about her. Her parents stopped coming around. She obviously wasn't hurting for any money, but this is just a modest neighborhood."

"So, her parents used to visit pretty regularly?"

"That was even longer ago. Probably a few years now. They used to come and visit with her. Sometimes they'd go inside and sometimes they'd go out somewhere. I met them one time, way back when they first bought the house. Before the girl was around. But, as I said, the neighborhood isn't exactly friendly. We don't go out of our way to make connections," she says.

"I remember," I nod. I reach into my pocket and pull out a card to slide through the door to her. "If you think of anything else, give me a call."

She looks at the card and closes the door without another word.

So much for me thinking we might have established a rapport.

CHAPTER EIGHTEEN

THE INSIDE OF MILEY'S HOUSE IS MUCH LIKE IT WAS THE LAST TIME I was here. Slumbering. The neighborhood gave me a little bit, but not much. If anything, it brought up even more questions and underscored ones I already had.

Obviously, her family was part of her life. Her parents used to come and see her.

But they didn't come back when they found out their daughter was killed? They didn't question that she was supposedly in the house when she obviously wasn't?

How could they not have come? How could they not have wondered?

The only explanation I can come to is that they knew. They know what's going on. But even then, what is it that they know?

I walk carefully through the house, trying to look at it as though

I haven't seen it before. It's easy to get so accustomed to surroundings you lose track of what you're seeing. Everything just looks the way you expect it to look, so much so that your mind begins to eliminate details that should be standing out. I want to catch those details and find what they could mean.

I'm still searching for something to explain the sound of the gunshot that brought the police into the house and broke open the reality of what was happening there. The Breyer detectives didn't know what they were going to find when they went into the house. They didn't even really know why they were there.

They were working on a tip from an anonymous source, who told them the girl who lived in that house was missing and implied she might be the dead woman found in the woods who'd been lying with no name for nine months. But when they got to the house, they had no reason to go inside. Much like with Marie's apartment, there was no probable cause, no justification for the police to enter.

All they could do was knock on the door and hope someone inside opened it. When no one did, they spoke to neighbors, they did everything they could, but there was nothing else. Not until they heard a gunshot and one of the detectives reacted the same way I would have. With a boot to the door and her gun drawn.

That's when they discovered the treasure trove of information inside. The clues pointed to this woman being not only the one who was found dead but also the person responsible for helping Jonah escape from prison. At least, one of the people responsible. From there, the case became mine and I've been trying to take it apart piece by piece ever since.

And it keeps bringing me right back here.

We've since discovered that the lights were on a remote activation, and the prevailing theory is still that the gunshot is on a speaker of some sort. Whoever triggered that sound remotely intended for Detective Simon to come into the house. The why, presumably, was so we could find more information about Miley Stanford's life—and that the woman living here was not actually Miley, but Serena.

But so far, we can't put the last of it together.

I go through each room and go over every inch, every corner. There are still canned goods sitting in her kitchen pantry and somehow, of everything, that gets to me. I can imagine her standing in their kind of looking over everything she had and trying to decide what she was going to eat. It's a small space, smaller than I would have expected it to be considering its placement in the kitchen. It means she would have had to turn around in a circle just to look over everything on the shelves.

I compulsively reach out and touch one of the cans. The shelf beneath it creaks slightly and I pull my hand away. The last thing I need to do is to start destroying bits of the house that is still essentially one giant piece of evidence.

The next room where anything new stands out to me is the bedroom. I've been in here so many times before. I've dug through her clothes and tried to imagine what it would be like to be one woman who could turn into so many. But this time when I sift through the articles of clothing looking for anything new to jump out at me, it's not the clothes that give up their secrets.

It's the ceiling.

A feather tumbles down onto my face from some unseen accessory on a shelf above the bar and when I look up to see where it came from, I notice a faint outline on the ceiling. It looks almost like someone painted over a picture frame, but after I look at it for a few seconds, I realize it isn't a frame. It's a door. The house has an attic.

A call-up to the local precinct, an hour, and a tremendous amount of noise later, all of Serena's clothes are out of the closet and on the bed, and the once-sealed attic door is open. One of the men in the department sent over tugs down a fairly rickety-looking wooden ladder that had been shoved out of sight when the door was sealed over.

"Are you going to be okay?" he asks. "Want me to go up before you?"

I give him an incredulous look and climb the ladder without dignifying him with a response. My first breath up in the attic tells me now what has been up here for a long time. It's dense with dust and the smell of cardboard, paper, and fabric. The heat from downstairs has risen up into the space only slightly, but the air is still cold.

Taking my phone out of my pocket, I turn on the flashlight feature and shine the bright beam around me. It's not a large attic and every inch of the space seems stacked with boxes, crates, furniture, and loose articles that were haphazardly stuffed into place.

"I need a couple of guys up here to start unloading all of this," I call down. "Spread the tarps out on the front lawn and start bringing everything out. I need everything documented and photographed."

"It's going to take some time for us to get the resources here to handle that," one of the two uniformed officers who came along with the cast of breaking into the attic tells me.

"Just put in the call."

A couple of hours later I'm covered in dust, my skin itching and stinging with untold layers of dust and dirt and who knows what else. But there's new excitement in my heart. For the first time in a while, the new questions that have sprung up in me aren't frustrating. They seem like they're opening a path rather than taking one away.

As the team continues to go through each article lined up on the blue tarps stretched across the grass, I go back inside. I have a feeling and I need to check it out. Peeling off my gloves, I go back into the pantry. I look around at the shelves, noticing the slight difference in the wood making up the ones lining two of the walls.

The third set of shelves is the one that creaked when I touched the can of peaches earlier. I take a picture of the shelves so I can show the contents and everything in its place, then start unloading the food. I stack it beside me on the floor so I can examine the shelves more carefully. They aren't particularly well constructed. I don't think they're going to tumble off the wall if I breathe on them too hard, but they also weren't built with the same type of consideration and craftsmanship as the other shelves.

I run my fingertips around the joints where the shelves meet the wall and feel that they are connected by basic screws. I call out to the people milling around the house to find out if anyone has a screwdriver. It takes a couple of moments to rustle one up, but soon I'm loosening at the screws of the top shelf. It comes down without hesitation and I make quick work of the next two. With them on the floor, I can clearly see this wall has about as much structural integrity as the ceiling of the closet had.

Fortunately, the demolition guys are still here, and it takes only a couple of blows with their sledgehammer to reveal the door that had been hidden out of sight.

"What is that?" one of them asks.

"If I don't miss my guess, that is a basement," I tell him.

Somewhere further in the house, I hear a groan and know the news of another entire room potentially full of further dirty, forgotten items to dig through has traveled to all the officers. They'll remember this fondly in many years when they look back on their rookie years and all the shit they were put through by the people with more notches on their belts.

Or they won't. Either way, it needs to get done.

Once the door is photographed, I turn the knob. The door gives me a little bit of trouble, not wanting to open after having been covered up for so long. But I finally force it open with a rough shove. The wood slides open with an eerie creak, revealing darkness beneath.

I take a breath and step down into the grim depths beneath the house. At least this time there's a light switch. It does little more than cast a hazy yellow glow on the bottom few steps and a couple of feet into the basement, but it's something.

I step down to the dirty cement floor and glance around.

"Holy hell."

CHAPTER NINETEEN

"Who were they?"

"I don't know what you want me to tell you," Jonah says.

"I want you to tell me the truth. Who were they? Because up until now I've been under the impression that Miley's parents were traveling throughout Europe and just having too good of a time to make it back here to deal with the tiny little detail of their only daughter's supposed death, later clarified to be disappearance and identity theft. But I'm getting a different feeling now. I was going through my Miley's house today and I discovered a way into a secret attic and a basement, both hidden behind drywall."

"What was in them?" he asks.

"Their lives," I tell him. "Everything from baby books and first ballet shoes to a framed high school diploma and dressers still full of underwear. Their entire lives had been picked up and stuffed into an attic or shoved down into a basement that was sealed over so no one would even know they existed. They didn't go traveling in Europe. They disappeared. And who does that sound like?"

"I didn't disappear," Jonah grumbles.

"That's funny, because nobody knew where the hell you were," I snap.

"They also thought I was dead," Jonah points out. "Don't think I'm not fully aware of how easily my family went from having two sons to an only child."

"No, Jonah, you're not fully aware. You have no idea what they went through. But as difficult as it is for you to wrap your head around, this isn't actually about you. Right now, I'm talking about Miley Stanford and her parents. I want to know who they are. Or were. Are they even alive?"

"Yes," he says forcefully. "They are alive."

"Then where are they? Who are they? What the hell is going on?" I demand.

"I don't want to talk about this," he huffs.

I scoff. "You don't want to talk about this? You don't get a fucking choice. You told me that you were going to be honest with me. That you were going to tell me the truth. And then I find out that all this was going on, and clearly you know about it. So, when does the whole truth-telling segment of this interaction come into play?"

"I did promise you I would be honest with you," Jonah says. "But what I said was that I would tell you the truth that I had to tell. These are not my truths to tell."

"Oh, stop with the bullshit. I'm not asking you to bear your soul to me and let all your true colors shine through. I want to know basic facts."

"It's not for me to tell," he insists. "This belongs to them."

"You don't care about anyone else," I say.

"That's not true," he fires back.

"Do you know how I know the significance of finding all of Miley's stuff along with her parents' in that basement and attic? How I know that means Myles and Holly didn't just throw their daughter away?" I ask.

"How?"

"Because your parents did the same for you."

"My parents disowned me," he says, his voice dropping lower.

"Your parents did what they had to do to survive. But they could have thrown everything of yours away. If they didn't care, they could have just tossed it out the window into a dumpster. Hell, if it had been me, I would have piled it up in the middle of the yard and had a bonfire. But they didn't. They took all of their reminders of you, everything, and filled up that little room in the attic of their house. Then they sealed it over, just like Myles and Holly did. They couldn't bear the thought of you not existing in their world anymore. Even if they had to hide you. Your parents loved you, Jonah. They kept your memory, even if you didn't deserve it."

I don't know if it's late at night or early in the morning when my phone rings and I see Sam's name across the screen. I pick it up, immediately looking back at the computer in front of me.

"Have you slept at all?" he asks.

"In general?" I ask.

"Recently," he clarifies.

"Not much," I admit. "Listen to this. You remember I told you about Myles and Holly Stanford? The parents of that girl Miley?"

"Yes," he says. "I remember. They are supposed to be traveling in Europe or somewhere and weren't able to come back."

"Yes, exactly," I tell him. "Supposedly being the operative word there. That never struck me as authentic. Turns out, it's not."

"What do you mean?" he asks.

I fill him in on everything that happened.

"I couldn't get anything out of Jonah, but I have everything that they squirreled away in their house to go on, so I've been doing research. As it turns out, Holly and Myles aren't the sweet, indulgent well-to-do parents we might have thought. I'm sure they had plenty of money and they definitely indulged their daughter, but they didn't work for it. They're career criminals."

"They aren't traveling through Europe. They're on the run," he muses.

"My thoughts exactly. And they can't come back because if they step foot on American soil, some pissed-off bounty hunter is going to throw a fishing net over their heads, attach them to the back of his truck, and drag them back to the police," I say.

"Damn," he mutters.

"To say the least," I say. "But the thing is, it doesn't explain Miley. Where is she? What happened to her? They just hopped on a plane likely with some very creatively crafted fake identification and headed off to travel the world so they could escape prosecution under the guise of traveling. Why would they come up with something so complicated for their daughter if she was with them? Why wouldn't they just say she was traveling with them? As it is, this looks extremely suspicious. They would have had to know that people would expect them to come back stateside when their daughter was reported missing. All this does is turn more attention to them."

"So, what now?" he asks.

"Now, we try to hunt them down," I tell him. "A bit easier said than done."

"It is a fairly big world out there."

"Yeah. Those singing Disney dolls are a bunch of liars," I say.

"Well, it's not nearly as exciting as dashing the full-hearted hopes and starry-eyed dreams of young children everywhere by debunking a beloved song, but I did make a little bit of progress in Marie's case."

That perks up my ears a little. "What happened?"

"We searched through that phone and traced all of the numbers in it. There weren't many and most of them were burners that had been disconnected. One of them was still active, but just rang repeatedly every time we called it. The next one went straight to voicemail, to a full inbox, but it did give us an important bit of information. A name."

"Who was it?"

"A drug dealer who just so happens to be sitting in prison right now."

I'm about to ask him more when my phone clicks, indicating a call coming in on the other line. I glance at the screen to see who I'll be calling back and notice it's Bellamy. We haven't spoken since the hotel, so I'm curious whether she's calling to try to make amends or if she has come up with a new litany of complaints to levy against me.

"Babe, give me just a minute. It's Bellamy."

"Okay."

I flash over to her call, but it takes only a few seconds for me to be back with him.

"Sam, I'm going to have to call you back."

"What's going on?"

"Finn Fielding is dead."

CHAPTER TWENTY

BELLAMY AND I ARE BOTH CLOSER TO CAMPUS THAN WE WERE WHEN she came to pick me up from Dean and Xavier's house. But it still feels like the drive is stretching on an impossible amount of time as I try to get to the address she gave me to meet her. When I finally get to the unfamiliar house, she's sitting in her car, her head leaned forward on the steering wheel. There are two police cars in the yard and other cars up at the front of the driveway almost tucked behind the house.

Her shoulders aren't shaking, but when she looks up at me, I can see how red and swollen her eyes are. She looks like she can't cry anymore. She climbs out of the car and drops into my arms. I don't say anything. There's no need. Right now, I just need to stand here with her and let her get herself together. Finally, she moves her head just enough that I can hear her barely audible whisper.

"I'm sorry."

"No, I'm sorry. There's nothing for you to be sorry for."

"Yes, there is," she says. "I didn't believe you. I didn't think that there was anything strange going on when Liza died."

"I didn't know if there was," I say. "But you were right, B. I was being selfish. I shouldn't have gone behind your back to satisfy my own hunch. You at least deserved to be let in on my suspicions."

"I guess we were both right," she chuckles bitterly. "I'm sorry for being so horrible to you."

"Stop," I admonish her with a sad smile. "You were not horrible to me. Now is not the time for you to be thinking about anything but your friends. You earned that right with a whole lot of years of being my best friend. Now, explain to me what's going on."

"We don't know," she says. "After I dropped you off, I went home. I checked in with everybody. Finn was saying he thought he might not do a funeral, that he would just have her cremated and then everybody could go to see the mausoleum when it was right for them. Of course, that caused a whole thing because a couple of the group thought that wasn't enough for her, and a couple others thought it was his choice and if the rest wanted to do something more to memorialize her, we could all get together for some drinks and dinner or a little gathering at the house. He pointed out the visitation at the sorority house was about as much funeral-type activity as he thought he could take.

"Anyway, he was getting upset, understandably, and stopped responding to everybody. Then he started texting us, just talking about what it was like when we were younger and all the time we were spending together."

"Oh, no," I whisper.

She draws in a shuddering breath. "A couple of nights ago, they all got together for dinner at Priscilla's house. They called and asked if I wanted to come, but I had some things I needed to take care of for work and around the house, then I was going to go to the hospital to see Eric and Bebe. I missed them so much I just wanted to be near them. So I said no. Then this morning Adam called him to check on him because he hadn't heard from him. They were supposed to get together this afternoon. When he didn't answer, Adam went over to the house and found him."

I've been trying so hard to just listen and let her say whatever it is she needs to say that the inconsistency doesn't hit me until right now.

"Wait… I think I'm confused. What does this have to do with how I reacted to Liza's death?" I ask. "If he killed himself…"

She shakes her head. "He died of the same thing."

"The same thing?" I gasp.

She nods. "When Adam found him, there were signs in the house that he had been throwing up and things had been knocked over, so it looks like he might have been dizzy and unsteady on his feet. His phone was near his hand and he had started to dial 911. That's why we're here, Emma. This doesn't make sense. I really wanted to think Liza's death was just a fluke. That it was just a tragedy.

"I think that's why I got as upset with you as I did. I didn't want to have to think about it anymore. Liza was so young and full of life. I didn't want to dig so deep into her death because I didn't want to know what was in there. I know, that goes against everything in my training. It goes against what you believe in. What I thought I believed in. But I just couldn't take it."

"I understand," I nod. "If there's anybody who understands something like that, it's me."

"But now that Finn is dead, it can't just be a coincidence. This is too suspicious. I need you to look into it. I need you to find out what he did to her," she says.

"Well, you know what we always say," I say.

"There is no such thing as coincidence," she replies sadly.

As soon as we step into the house, we are immersed in chaos. Voices seem to be shouting from every room, and in the living room to one side, I see a haggard-looking detective trying to simultaneously scribble notes on a pad in his hand and respond to the woman shouting at him.

It takes a second for me to realize the shouting woman is Regan. I go into the room and a uniformed officer immediately steps into my path.

"No," he says. "They're enough people in here already. Everybody needs to get out."

I reach into my pocket and pull out my shield, holding it up to show him. "Everybody but me."

"Oh, shit. Chief already called in the feds?"

"No," I tell him. "I'm here unofficially. But it seems you've lost control of your scene. If you want my help, I'll pull the reins back for you."

He looks over at the detective, who swings his hand open in front of him like he's giving me an invitation.

"Be my guest," he says.

I clear my throat.

"I need everybody in here!" I shout. "Everybody in the house, uniform or not, needs to come into the living room now."

That seems to cut through the chaos. The house falls silent and all eyes turn to me.

"This is now an active scene. I need everyone to account for where you've been in the house. I want to know every room you went in, everything you touched, everything you saw. I'm going to start collecting suspects if I feel like one of you is hiding something from me."

That's all it takes for the room to fill with police and the group of friends. They scatter around on the furniture in the room or in the case of the officers, stand at the edges of the room.

"What's going on?" Adam whispers. "What's she doing here again?"

"I called her," Bellamy explains. "Emma is the best of the best. She's the only one of us who was looking hard enough at the reality of what happened to Liza to think something was off about it. Or at least to think that someone should take the right steps to find out how she died. The rest of us were too busy telling stupid stories and fawning on Finn."

"His wife had just died," Regan says.

"And now he's dead, too," Bellamy points out. "And everything points to it being the same thing that killed both of them. Do you think that's a coincidence? Because I'm having a really hard time rationalizing that."

"What are you saying?" Maya asks.

"You know what she's saying," Adam says. "She thinks Finn murdered Liza."

"And then killed himself," Regan adds.

Adam looks down at his hands, rocking back and forth on the couch like he's doing everything he can to keep from crying. Regan quickly moves over beside him and wraps her arm around him. She rests her head against his shoulder and he leans toward her. Maya sits down on his other side and reaches for his hand. Soon Priscilla joins in, sitting on her knees on the floor in front of Regan so that she can lean against her.

I look around for Darren and find him standing at the window, staring outside like he's not even there. He's disconnected himself and I'm curious why.

"Darren?" I ask. He turns to look at me but doesn't say anything. "You haven't said much."

"What is there to say?"

"Do you," I look at the others, "any of you, know of anything that was going on between Liza and Finn?"

They all shake their heads and exchange glances like they are trying to figure out if one of them knows something and hasn't told the rest.

"Are you sure?" Bellamy asks. "All of you were around them far more than I was, so you're going to know more. I thought they looked like they were doing really well. They seemed really happy the last time I saw them. But was there something happening the investigators should know about?"

"If you can find her journal, that might help," Regan offers.

"Journal?" I ask.

The women all nod.

"She journaled every day. It was something she started doing in college," Priscilla explains.

"She went through a really rough patch of depression and her therapist said that journaling could help her to get better in touch with her thoughts and emotions," Bellamy says.

"I am very familiar with that recommendation," I say.

"Well, Liza took it really seriously. Once she started back then, she said it totally changed her life and she hasn't stopped. Hadn't stopped."

"So, if there is something we need to know about their relationship, it's going to be in those journals," I muse.

Bellamy nods.

I look at the detective. "These are longtime friends of the deceased. Both of them. Will you give permission for them to look for the journals? Or do you need a search warrant?"

CHAPTER TWENTY-ONE

"She was having an affair," Priscilla says, her voice powdery like she can barely even bring herself to form the words.

"How could she do that to Finn?" Regan asks. "They were so happy together. He was so good to her."

"As far as we know," Bellamy counters.

"What is that supposed to mean?" Maya asks.

"I'm just saying we only know what they showed us. All we can really see about their relationship is what they chose to present to the outside world. I know we were close to them, but that doesn't mean we know everything about them. Obviously, they were having problems of some kind. It's all the right there in her journals," Bellamy says.

We left Finn and Liza's house and have moved to Priscilla's home just a few blocks away to go through the journals we found in the bedroom. Being there in the space where Finn had just died and where something befell Liza just days ago was a heavy feeling. The home had taken on the same kind of tension as Miley's house in the earliest days of that investigation. It still hadn't figured out it was empty. That those who had filled it with energy and life would never be back.

The reminders of them and the lives they lived were all around. It was more than just the Thanksgiving dishes sitting in the dining room and on the kitchen counter. Those were hard to look at, but they had enough distance they could still be abstract.

It's always hard to think about those who have been lost missing out on everything that continues on even after they die. Knowing Liza will never cook that Thanksgiving dinner and Finn will never eat it is difficult. But it's the reminders of the mundane that are considerably more challenging to cope with.

Everywhere in the house, there were signs of these two people simply living. Not preparing for anything big. Not dealing with anything painful and challenging. Just… living.

There's a load of laundry still in the washing machine, ready to be changed over to the dryer. Another sits, already sorted out, in a basket on the floor beside the machines. The smell of their last days still lingers in the air. Cold stale coffee mixed with a fresher pot. Sweet vanilla and spicy black pepper. Aftershave and soap.

One of Liza's slippers is shoved under the edge of the couch and the other sits in the middle of the room, like she'd taken them off and accidentally kicked one of them. Finn's pajamas from the night before were still balled up on the floor of the bedroom.

Moving over to Priscilla's house got us away from those reminders so we can talk more clearly. The detectives came with us, but have stayed out of the conversation, choosing instead to observe and take notes.

"So, it's Finn's fault that she cheated on him?" Darren asks. "Is that what you're saying?"

"No," Bellamy replies. "That's not what I'm saying. It's obviously not his fault she cheated on him. Choosing to have an affair is absolutely on her. But it's naive to think everything was perfect between them and then all of a sudden she just decided to go sleep with some guy. That doesn't happen."

"Finn was good to her," Regan insists. "He loved her. He has since college."

"Guys," Priscilla says. "We can't just not talk about it."

"Not talk about what?" I ask.

They all look at each other, each seeming reluctant to be the one to speak up. Unspoken emotions pass back and forth through the group, as if they're trying to silently elect an official representative to be the one to put the voice to the words none of them want to say. Finally, it falls on Bellamy. It seems she's going to be the liaison between them and me, their world and the one outside of them.

"Liza suspected that Finn had an affair early in their marriage," she explains. "There wasn't any proof really, and they never confirmed it, but it really got to her. It caused some serious tension in their marriage. For a while there I didn't know if they were going to make it."

"But they did," Adam adds. "Even though Finn would never admit to cheating on her, he agreed to go to counseling and they both said they came out of that better than ever."

"Then why would she turn around and have an affair?" I ask.

"You've never made a mistake?" Maya raises an eyebrow.

"This isn't about me," I say. "This is about trying to understand what happened to your two friends. Both of whom are dead, by the way. Just in case you've forgotten."

"Emma," Bellamy says in that voice that means I need to dial it back.

"We haven't forgotten," Darren tells me. "And if you are going to just stand there and attack us, and accuse all of us of things you don't know anything about, maybe you shouldn't be around."

"I'm not accusing anybody of anything," I say. "If anything, all these journals indicate is exactly what the suspicions were in the first place. Liza did not die of an illness or an infection. She was murdered. Finn found out she was having an affair, or likely already knew and was hoping it would stop, but it didn't. He was angry and killed her."

"But then why would he kill himself?" Maya asks. "If he was so mad at her for having an affair that he was willing to murder her, why would he turn around and commit suicide because he was so upset she was gone?"

"Haven't you ever made a mistake?" I ask.

The woman's eyes narrow at me. "Not one like that."

"The point is, people do things they regret all the time. He could have been so furious and sickened by her in one moment that all he could think about was punishing her and taking away his pain. Maybe even hurting the man she was cheating on him with by taking her away from him. But then when she was gone, the anger disappeared, and he realized what he had done, he was so distraught he couldn't live with himself," I postulate.

"But this doesn't seem like a spur-of-the-moment thing," Darren says. "He didn't shoot her or strangle her."

Maya shudders and pushes closer to Adam, like sitting close to him will give her enough strength to get through the rest of the conversation.

"We don't know what happened to her. Or to him," I nod.

"Exactly," Regan says. "This was something he planned. He thought about it enough that he was able to kill her without anyone realizing it was murder. Then he offed himself in the same way as... what? Some sort of penance?"

"There is another possibility," I offer.

"What?" Priscilla asks.

"I know the easiest answer is that he killed her and then killed himself because he felt guilty about it. But he may have killed himself because he knew the method he chose wasn't perfect. That someone was going to figure out what he did, and he would have to face the consequences for it. It's a lot easier for people to wrap their heads around the possibility of killing someone when they don't think there will be any repercussions. But as soon as they realize the people around them will know what they did and they will have to face up to it, it's no longer an option. Or, if they have already done it, the benefits of living that way no longer outweigh the detractions," I explain.

"The autopsy," Bellamy says.

I nod at her. "Not having an autopsy makes it a hell of a lot harder to detect subtle methods of murder."

"No," Maya says, shaking her head. "Finn has never believed in autopsies. Don't you remember when his grandmother died? His grandfather insisted on an autopsy even though the woman was ninety-eight years old. The whole thing was traumatizing for Finn. He couldn't stand the idea of them cutting open his grandmother. There was never going to be a time when he would agree to have his wife treated in the same way."

"Which might just support that claim rather than prove it wrong," Adam chimes in. "Think about it. In the rest of your life, outside of Finn, have you ever met anyone who has a strong opinion about something like an autopsy? Some people have strong opinions one way or the other about organ donation. Or about living donations. About blood transfusions. But have you ever heard anybody get so heated about not agreeing with compulsory autopsies?"

"No," Maya admits.

"No," Regan agrees.

"And everybody knows it about him. It's so weird it stands out. That's one of those fun facts somebody might share about him in a class," Adam continues.

"Not exactly a fun fact," Darren points out.

"Maybe not, but something distinctive nonetheless. And if he already knew that none of us would think twice about him turning down an autopsy comment it would just give him an avenue. All he would need to do was figure out a way to kill her that wouldn't look suspicious enough for the police to get involved so he could turn down the autopsy, play the grieving widower, and move on with his life," Adam says.

"With the proceeds of a lawyer's life insurance," Regan adds.

Priscilla stands up, rubbing her arms like she's suddenly cold. "This entire conversation is disturbing. I feel like all of you think we're playing a game of *Clue*. Have you forgotten that these are our friends? Were our friends? And both of them are dead?"

"Nobody has forgotten that, Priscilla," Bellamy tells her.

"It seems like all of them have," she says.

"She's right," Maya says. "Listen to us. We're all coming up with these stories rather than actually trying to figure out what happened."

"Does it really matter what happened?" Regan asks. "They're both dead. It's not like either one of them will go to trial. There's no battling over the life insurance."

"That's true," I acknowledge. "But even when a situation looks like a clear case of murder-suicide, investigators can't just close the book on it and say they're done. There still has to be an investigation. There has to be proof of what happened and how. There's no suicide note claiming responsibility, so automatically making the official legal finding that he killed her and himself could be considered slander. I mean, that is our easy motive, but it's also possible that this was never murder at all. That's why we need to find the truth."

"What about the journals?" Darren ask.

"They were her journals, not his. Even though they create motive, it's not enough. There's nowhere in those journals that Liza ever said she was afraid of Finn, or that he ever hurt her. She doesn't talk about them arguing or even their relationship being bad. There are a couple of times where she talks about things between them not being like they used to be, but that's nothing. If longing for better times or lamenting the loss of intense passion in a relationship was grounds for murder, we'd wipe out a good chunk of the population. And a rather significant segment of the music industry," I say. "The point is, people who are together for a long time go through cooling-off phases sometimes. That's not an immediate reason to kill, and it doesn't give investigators the right to rubberstamp a situation."

"So what does that mean for us?" Adam asks. "What do we do?"

"It means we need to put the pieces together. Connect the dots. We need to figure out exactly what happened and how so we all know," Bellamy tells him. "And so both of them can rest."

CHAPTER TWENTY-TWO

THE DETECTIVES ARE STILL HOVERING AT THE EDGE OF THE ROOM, watching intently but not saying anything. They haven't disconnected. I can tell by the way they're watching each of the members of the friend group they are trying to make sense of the situation. By figuring out their personalities and how they communicate best, the detectives can determine how to approach each of these people if they think they might have information.

I glance their way to acknowledge them, then continue on.

"The first thing we need to do is figure out where everybody was the last couple of days," I say.

"Why would you need to know where we were?" Priscilla asks.

"Tracing movement helps to establish a timeline," I explain. "If one of you happened to see either Liza or Finn somewhere close to the time of their death, it can narrow it down if there are movements to better pinpoint exactly what happened when."

"The medical examiner says Finn died sometime late last night," Detective Gabriel pipes up. "They haven't been able to give an exact time because he died near the fireplace, so it threw off the temperature of his body."

"Alright," I nod. "That helps. That means whatever happened was some time after he came home after doing whatever he was doing yesterday evening. He had enough time to come inside, start a fire. When did all of you see him last?"

"At dinner," Maya says.

Bellamy looks over at me. "Remember, I told you they all got together for dinner the night before last."

"Here. I cooked," Priscilla says. "It's something we used to do together a lot before our lives got busier. We would come together at one of our houses at least twice a month for a big dinner. It had kind of fallen by the wayside, but I thought considering the circumstances, now would be a good time to try to reinstate it."

"It was a really beautiful idea," Maya says, rubbing her arm gently.

"How did he act at dinner?" I ask.

"Pretty much like you would expect a man to act after he just lost his wife," Darren comments.

"That's the thing," I say. "There isn't one way people act. A lot of times you hear that somebody is obviously guilty for doing something because they don't have enough emotion after a death. Or they have too much emotion after a death. They do or don't say the right things to the right person at a specific time. They are too active or not active at all. But every person is different. Every person handles grief differently. Just because you handled grief one way in one situation doesn't mean that's the way you're going to handle it in another situation. Until you have experienced that moment of loss, you have no idea how you're going to react."

"He was upset," Maya tells me. "Anxious."

"Anxious?" I ask. "Was that normal for him?"

"Not really," Priscilla says. "He wasn't really a very high-strung person. But obviously, we were giving him some grace because of what was going on."

"And he said he wasn't sleeping," Regan adds. "But he hadn't slept since Liza died."

"That's right," Adam nods. "He was drinking a ton of coffee. It was like he was fighting with himself not to fall asleep. Like if he fell asleep, somehow it would be more real."

"I know that feeling," I tell him. "I know exactly what he meant. When my mother was murdered, my father said he didn't want to sleep. Not that he couldn't, but that he didn't want to. Because if he laid down and went to sleep, he was accepting that the next day he would wake up and she would be gone. As long as he could stay awake, he could pretend it was the same day and she was still somewhere. Or at least that his life wasn't moving forward without her."

"That doesn't sound like a man so infuriated with his wife he would want her dead," Regan muses.

"Or exactly like a man who couldn't stand what he did to the woman he loved so much," Darren counters.

"When he drank his coffee, was it something he brought with him?" I ask.

"No," Maya shakes her head. "We've always had a ton of coffee around when we have dinner."

"I'm a bit of a coffee fiend," Regan admits. "It helps when you know the person roasting the beans."

"That would be me," Darren says.

"Really?" I ask. "I've never known anybody who roasts coffee beans before."

"He's incredible at it," Priscilla tells me. "He makes the most delicious blends."

"All of us have gotten a little bit addicted over the years," Maya says. "He likes to use us as guinea pigs. And of course, every holiday and birthday we know exactly what we're getting."

"Not that any of us mind," Adam says. "Darren has created a different roast for all of us."

The big, quiet man looks like he is uncomfortable, like he doesn't want to be the center of this conversation.

"Do you have any of it around?" I ask.

Everybody looks at Priscilla, who nods. "I'm pretty sure I do. Let me go check the kitchen."

I follow after her and watch as she takes a small wooden crate out of one of the cabinets. She turns around and jumps slightly when she sees me.

"I'm sorry, I didn't mean to startle you," I say.

"It's alright. With all this going on, I'm just a little bit jumpy," she says.

"That's understandable," I tell her. "Is this it? This is the exact coffee that you served at dinner the other night?"

"Yes. The same bag, actually."

I look into the crate. The bag of coffee sits on a bed of what looks like shredded brown cardboard. Then up against it is a small burlap sack.

"What's that?" I point.

"Flavored sugar cubes," she says. "Darren includes those with every bag of coffee. They're supposed to compliment the flavor of the beans."

"And everybody drank coffee that night?" I ask.

"Yeah," she confirms. "We like to joke that we know we've gotten old because the college friends we used to sit around and drink liquor with we now sit around and drink coffee with."

"I know the feeling," I tell her. "And you think that Finn drank more coffee than he usually does?"

"Not a huge amount more. Maybe an extra cup or two," she shrugs.

"Okay. Thank you."

I hand the crate back and return to the living room with the rest of them.

"I wanted to tell you he was at my house last night," Darren announces.

"He was?" Maya frowns. "I wasn't able to get in touch with him at all."

"When he was over, he said he left his phone in the car. He didn't stay for long. He came over and said he needed to talk. He talked about Liza for a while. We had a couple of drinks."

"What kind of drinks?" I ask.

"I had a beer and he had tea. He said his throat had been bothering him and maybe he was getting sick. I think it was just from him crying. But he asked if I had any hot tea, so I made him some. He drank almost a cup of it, we talked, and then he left. He was upset, but he didn't seem too agitated. He was calmer than he was at dinner. We made plans to go fishing this afternoon with Adam," he says.

"Fishing in the afternoon?" I ask.

Adam lets out a short laugh. "For Finn, fishing was mostly just floating around on a boat or sitting on the bank of the river, eating sandwiches, and relaxing. He didn't like to go early in the morning because it was too cold. He brought in a couple little guppies sometimes, but I don't know if he would know what to do with himself if he actually caught a regular size fish."

"So, what's going to happen now?" Regan asks.

Once again, all eyes turn to me.

"Right now, there are still so many questions, the investigation is primarily exploratory. Toxicology takes a couple of weeks to come back, so we can't necessarily depend on the result of that to get us all our answers unless there's no other avenue. If Detective Gabriel feels the situation warrants it, the crime scene investigation unit can go to the house and check around, see if they can identify anything that might have contributed to the deaths."

"So, basically what you're saying is we wait," Maya sighs.

"Essentially," I say. "We wait and we hope for the best."

CHAPTER TWENTY-THREE

"What did the police think?" Dean asks on our video call later.

"They are definitely leaning toward the murder-suicide possibility. It's what makes the most sense with the information we have right now. It seemed strange to me how surprised their friends were about the affair. I know it's not something everybody talks about, but I feel like at least one of the women in the group would have known. That's a lot to carry around without anybody to talk to about it or get support from," I tell him.

"Well, maybe that's just the issue," Dean offers. "Maybe she was looking for support but knew she wasn't going to get it from any of the friend group because her husband was also friends with them. That can be a really awkward situation. Maybe she just didn't want to face it."

"What about the cause of death?" Xavier chimes in. "Any more idea now that you can add his death to the mix?"

"Nothing concrete," I reply. "Because nobody was with him at the time he died, we don't really know what symptoms he was experiencing. All we know for sure is he was vomiting. The things knocked over in the house and possibly even him falling asleep in front of the fireplace could indicate that he was stumbling or disoriented. That's purely conjecture, but it does seem like it is the same cause of death as Liza."

"And we're pretty sure it's not bubonic plague?"

"Yes, Xavier. We're pretty sure it's not bubonic plague."

"That's pretty disappointing," he sighs. "Not that I would wish the plague on anyone, especially a friend of a friend… of a friend. But it would have been exciting to have been tangentially involved in one of the very rare cases of Black Death." A slow sigh slips out of his lungs. "I guess that leaves us with arsenic."

"Just like that?" I raise an eyebrow. "That leaves us with arsenic?"

"Well, that is the method of poisoning that seems the most likely. Since I'm not familiar with any cases where somebody managed to commit both murder and suicide by means of difficult to detect infectious disease, I would think poisoning would seem like the most logical option."

"That actually is logical," I say. "I had considered poisoning, but that's not my area of expertise."

"Me neither," he shrugs. "But arsenic poisoning was the murder methodology of choice for disgruntled, overzealous social climbers, and insurance fraudsters and the like back in the day."

"Gotta love an equal opportunity poison," I remark.

"I wouldn't necessarily say equal opportunity. It was overwhelmingly used by women. But one of the most popular things about it was it was almost impossible to detect. During those times, illness was rampant, and it was incredibly easy to contract a foodborne infection. The somewhat slapdash approach to food sanitation and freshness, as well as overall neglect in areas such as washing their hands and refrigeration, made eating a fairly prickly proposition. A basic meal was like a game of Russian roulette.

"To the dastardly benefit of our murderers, the symptoms of arsenic poisoning mimicked that of foodborne infection as well as a pantheon of popular illnesses of the day, including our old friend cholera. Women could look to the outside like they were doting wives and nurses, fawning over family members, friends, wealthy beneficiaries, the guy down the street who they thought might be fun to kill, pretty much anybody. But what they were actually doing was continuously dosing their victims with poison through their food and drinks.

"Consider the infamous case of Madame Lafarge. In 1840 she was brought to trial, accused of murdering her husband. She was only twenty-three years old at the time and a year before she had been forced into marriage to one Charles Lafarge. He had presented himself as being a very rich ironworker, but after the marriage, she discovered he was actually bankrupt.

"While Charles was on business, his wife mailed him a cake. He undoubtedly thought this was a token of her love and ate it eagerly. He promptly fell extremely ill. He spent two weeks sick at home with his wife showering him with attention, bringing him food and even his favorite beverage, eggnog. It wasn't even Christmas, but I digress.

"Charles died at the end of those two weeks and most simply thought he'd gotten an illness while away or had a foodborne infection. Some suspicious police, however, believed he was poisoned. They had his vomit and stomach examined, arsenic was identified, and his wife was brought up on charges. The entire trial was a circus. A parade of scientists and doctors came in attempting to either prove or disprove that Charles Lafarge died of arsenic poisoning.

"They employed several different methods, including one referred to as the Marsh test. A sample believed to contain arsenic, such as food or drink or a piece of tissue from a corpse, is mixed with acid and zinc. This creates a gas that should create a metallic film if exposed to a porcelain plate. The scientist who created the test proclaimed it to be irrefutable and capable of detecting even the smallest traces of arsenic in whatever was tested.

"Which sounded great, until the different times the test was performed produced different results because the people using it weren't actually trained in how to do the test or how to read the results. They ended up testing the eggnog and found arsenic there, but not actually in some of Charles's intestines. Which caused the defense to state that evidence couldn't be used to prove that the arsenic killed him because it was in the food and not the body, so maybe the eggnog was just poison.

"Anyway, long story short, they kept running out of samples of the body to test, so they ended up exhuming his body and taking pieces of his partially decomposed insides and tissues and dissecting them in the courtroom. Eventually, the court accepted the testimony of a scientist trained in the use and analysis of the Marsh apparatus that, in fact, arsenic was present in the exhumed Lafarge goo. Madame was found guilty and sentenced to life. But there were plenty of people who believed she was innocent and found guilty only because of reliance on notoriously unreliable and potentially witchcrafty science.

"I might have added the witchcrafty part to that, but it seems like it fits the mood. And the general overwrought religious slant to the majority of perceptions of the time. And lack of science."

Dean and I stare at Xavier for a few seconds after he finishes talking just to make sure that he's actually done. My cousin's eyes swing over to me.

"I'm certainly glad he isn't an expert," he says.

"I'm just glad Sam isn't here," I say.

CHAPTER TWENTY-FOUR

Sam

Sam walked into the stark cement room and stared at the man sitting shackled to a metal table bolted to the floor. His bright red jumpsuit marked him as one of the most dangerous inmates in the prison. Sam had no idea what had earned the man that red jumpsuit, or even the specifics of why he was in the prison. He also didn't care.

All that mattered to him was that this man's contact information had shown up on the phone in his cousin Marie's apartment.

He sat down across from him and set a manila envelope on the table between them. Taking a second to look into the man's eyes, he folded his hands on the table in front of him.

"Gerard Collins," he started.

"Yeah," the man said. "And who are you?"

"Sheriff Samuel Johnson," he said.

Collins smirked. "Sheriff? I didn't know we had any o' those around here. Shouldn't you be wearing a cowboy hat and gnawing on a piece of straw? Maybe polishing up your spurs?"

"How do you know Marie Johnson?"

"Marie?" Collins asked. "I don't know no Marie. Did you say Johnson? Like your name? Is this your old lady?"

Collins was leaned back in the chair, his sagging posture saying he didn't give a damn what was happening. Time behind bars didn't mean much to him. It was all but inevitable where he came from. From the moment he'd been born, a countdown clock had been hovering over him. The seconds ticked away, counting down his life until he followed in the footsteps of virtually all the men in his family who came before him. The only ones who hadn't ended up in prison were the ones who ended up dead first.

This was just a step on the path he already knew he was following. When he was growing up, there was no such thing as looking ahead to the future he wanted to make for himself. He never had dreams of what he wanted to be or what he was going to achieve. All he could do was follow the path that had been laid out for him.

It didn't matter how many times he was dragged into jail or how much more time got tacked on with every new sentence. Even getting released didn't matter. He saw it as a nice break. A diversion. That was his version of a vacation. In the end, the prison was always going to be home. He would always end up back.

But that didn't mean he was just going to cop to anything people blamed him for. He owned up to what he did. He wasn't going to lie, sometimes he was even proud of it. A lot of times he was proud of it. But that meant he wasn't going to take the fall for somebody else who should have had to deal with it on his own. There was no point in that. No honor in it.

"Stop the lying bullshit, Collins. It's not going to get you anywhere. I want to know how you met Marie and what you know about her," Sam snapped.

"I told you, I don't know no Marie. Not Marie Johnson. Not Marie anything. So, why don't you go find Opie and do some fishin' or some shit and leave me alone."

Sam slammed his hands on the table in front of him.

"Stop lying! Your contact information was in a phone found in her apartment. She lives alone. What does that tell you? Because it tells me she had contact with you right up until you landed your sorry ass in here. And she didn't even know you were here because she tried to call you a few more times. So, I'm going to try this again. What do you know about Marie?"

He didn't mean to intimidate Collins. He hadn't even planned on doing it. There was just so much anger and frustration flooding through him he couldn't contain it. The sound seemed to both startle and impress the inmate. It was like something clicked in him and he could suddenly connect with Sam's pain.

"Look, I... I ain't trying to jerk you around. I don't know her." He pauses like he's thinking through something. "She go by anything else?"

"Why would she go by anything else?" Sam asked. "That's her name. She's not that kind of person."

Collins snorted out a laugh and shook his head. "Anybody in here not wearing a uniform and everybody out there calls me Rocky. You think my mama went to Philly and got with a boxer?"

Sam took what the man in front of him said and used it to approach him from a different angle, taking a leap and hoping it paid off.

"Maybe she just thought you looked like a squirrel when you were born," he said.

Collins looked at him for a second, then chuckled.

"Hey, I get it. Like Bullwinkle. I feel you. My Gramps and I used to watch all those old shows together all the time," he said. A few seconds passed in silence before Sam felt a shift in the air. Collins looked at him again. "Who is this chick you're asking about?"

"Her name is Marie Johnson. She's my cousin."

"Your cousin?" he raised an eyebrow.

"Yeah. My little cousin. She's a grown woman, but I grew up with her like my sister."

This struck a chord. Collins straightened up and leaned toward Sam.

"I got one of those, too. Something happen to her?"

"I hope not. She's been missing."

"Missing? Shit." He thought for another second. "I don't mean no disrespect by this, but you got to stop thinking about her the way you remember when she was little. If she has my phone number, she is the kind of person who goes by something else. Feel me?"

"I don't know of anything else she'd go by," Sam told him. "I didn't know anything like this was going on in her life. Not until she disappeared."

"You got a picture?" Collins asked.

Sam took out a snapshot of Marie from the wedding.

"This is at my wedding," he said. "Last year."

He hoped something would spark in Collins. That seeing her face would bring out some kind of recognition. But it didn't seem to. He just kept looking at the picture and shaking his head.

"I don't know her. I wish I did. I wish I could tell you something. Sometimes my people use my phone. I can ask around. See if I can find out anything. But you best not let anyone know I'm helping a Sheriff."

The words sounded somewhere between threatening and joking, so Sam nodded. He'd appreciate anything this man could find out for him. He didn't know if he fully believed him. He was much more inclined to think that he did know Marie and just didn't want to admit it. But he'd hang on to any hope that may exist.

"Thanks, Rocky."

CHAPTER TWENTY-FIVE

"Emma, please, I need you to come now."

I might have actually been asleep, but it's been so long since I've slept more than a few minutes at a time, I might also have forgotten what that's like. The voice is coming at me from where a ringing used to be, so I think I answered the phone.

"Bellamy?"

I don't understand why I'm hearing her voice come through a phone. We decided to stay in the area for a few days and are sharing a room. The last I knew, she was asleep in the other bed.

"Emma, please."

She sounds desperate enough to cut through all the fog and get me sitting up. I don't know what's going on, but I'm already on my feet, headed for the dresser to pull out clothes.

"What's happening? What's wrong?"

"It's Darren," she says.

"Darren?"

"He's in the hospital."

"I'm on my way," I say.

"I'm right outside."

My head is spinning as I dress as fast as I can and run outside. Bellamy's hands grip the steering wheel so tightly her knuckles are turning white.

"When did you leave?" I ask.

"Maya called me a couple hours ago. You had finally fallen asleep, so I didn't want to disturb you."

"What's going on?"

The car is already racing back in the direction of the hospital. I brace myself for what I'm about to hear. It's a strange situation to be in, where I am actually hoping for some sort of accident or injury. Maybe this is the moment for an infectious disease to show up.

But I know that's not what's happening. I know what she's going to say.

"He was at work and started feeling sick. He got really dizzy and disoriented and said he was sick to his stomach. He was feeling so bad, he didn't think that he could drive to get to the doctor, so he called Maya. She is the one of the group who works closest to his workshop, so he asked if she would come get him and bring him to the hospital. She was only a few minutes away, but by the time she got to him, he had collapsed."

"Was he alone?"

"He only has two people who work for him and just one of them was there today. She said when she came in, he was already complaining about not feeling well and he went into his office pretty immediately after she got there. He said she should hold down the fort because he was going to have to take the rest of the day off. He was just feeling so sick. When Maya got there, he was on the floor in his office."

"Shit," I mutter.

"What is going on, Emma?"

I shake my head slightly. "I don't know." I think about the conversation I had with Xavier and Dean. I don't know if I want to tell Bellamy about it. I don't want to upset her more than she already is. At the same time, not having any idea what's going on might be worse. "Xavier thinks it sounds like arsenic poisoning."

She gives a quick intake of breath and her hands tighten even more on the steering wheel.

"How? How would they have all been exposed to arsenic?" she asks. "Does that mean it could have been an accident?" She flashes a fast look in my direction. "Maybe Finn and Liza didn't die the way we thought. If it's arsenic, it could have been an accident. Isn't arsenic in all sorts of things like ant killer?"

"I don't think they use arsenic in normal household pesticides and things anymore," I tell her. "They definitely used to, but I think that was phased out a long time ago. I guess it could be found in other products." I take out my phone to look it up. It only takes a few moments to find an answer. "It's still found in commercial products, especially pesticides used to treat imported lumber to protect it from decay. Were Finn and Liza doing any kind of home improvement work or building or anything?"

"Yes," she nods. "They were building a new deck."

I wish I hadn't mentioned the possibility to her. She's perking up and I'm not confident enough in the theory for her to be basing that kind of emotion on it. Bellamy hasn't been working with the Bureau as long as I have. She knows good and well how damaging it can be for those in the midst of a death or disappearance investigation to not have any hope. What I've learned in my time in the field—a kind of work she's never done—is how damaging it can be when they have too much.

It's not that I don't want her to be hopeful or optimistic. I know that this is a devastating situation and she is trying her hardest to navigate it and cope with everything that seems to be happening so fast around her. I want more than anything for there to be some sort of resolution that is less painful. Something that would somehow make this less horrible. Maybe if the deaths were accidents rather than something purposeful that was done by one of her dear friends to another, it would be easier.

But I don't know if that's what happened. I'm leaning toward no. It would be too much of a coincidence. Especially without a clear explanation. An accidental death to one person might slip through and be difficult to detect. Two people is harder. Adding a third person falling severely ill of apparently the same cause, but in a different time and place, and the leap that it takes to make an accident plausible is extreme, to say the least.

It's not completely impossible. There's a chance Darren was helping Finn and Liza with their project, was exposed to the same contaminant, and simply began experiencing symptoms at a later time. The different timelines could have to do with how much of the poison they were exposed to or how. It is technically possible. But the chances are slim, and I don't want to think Bellamy is getting herself built up for the possibility only to be crushed down harder when she finds the truth.

And I am determined to find the truth.

We get to the hospital and have barely gotten through the doors to the ward where Darren is receiving treatment when I can hear angry voices. It's reminiscent of the day we went to Finn's house to deal with the aftermath of his death. Again, the friend group is angrily confronting the police. Only this time, there is a heavy air of suspicion and betrayal hanging over them.

"You," Maya snaps angrily when she notices me come into the hallway. Stepping around the police officer, she stalks toward me. "This is your fault."

"How is this my fault?" I protest. "Nobody even knows what happened."

"And you said you did," she accuses. "You said Finn killed Liza and then committed suicide. And now this. This happened because of you."

"You can't blame Emma," Bellamy says, trying to step in between us. "You can't blame anyone until we know what killed Liza and Finn, and what is making Darren so sick."

"Well, the doctors won't tell us anything," Adam says. "We've been trying to get information from them, but they are just refusing."

Maya walks up to him and wraps her arms around him, pressing her head into his chest like she is both comforting him and trying to get comfort for herself. He pats her back a few times, then his hand drops away in a gesture that says he's done with the affection, but she doesn't catch on. Or she doesn't care. She stays where she is for a few more seconds before he pulls himself away from her to come over to us.

"Is there anything you can do?" he asks. "They won't even tell us if he's still alive. None of us are related to him, so they won't tell us anything or let us go into the room. I know you aren't investigating him, but do you think you can at least find something out for us?"

"I'll see what I can do," I tell them.

I go to the nurse's station in the center of the floor and ask if Darren is being attended by Samantha Kelsey. It turns out she is leading his medical team, so I ask the nurse to have her paged and tell her I need to speak with her.

The long wait for Dr. Kelsey to get to me pairs with the exhausted, strained look on her face when she turns around the corner. She's trying to fight her hair back up into a clip at the back of her head and has traded the crisp clothing she'd been wearing the last time we spoke for scrubs.

"Agent Griffin," she greets me. "I thought I might see you here."

I nod. "Darren O'Malley."

"I have to admit, I was shocked when he showed up this morning. I remember him being here when Liza was fighting for her life and then when her husband came to speak to us about her body, he was with them as well."

"I'm sure you've heard what happened," I tell her.

She nods. "I did. I was actually just asked to submit details about my care of Liza to support the potential new criminal case."

"I didn't start the investigation," I say quickly.

"I know. But I'm sure you aren't fighting against it, either."

"No. I'm not. Something is happening here. You know it as well as I do. I thought it might be a murder-suicide. We uncovered some journals that gave information about Liza having an affair."

"That would make sense. Unfortunately, I've seen that more than my fair share of times," the doctor says.

"But now Darren. That doesn't make sense," I say. "Can you tell me about what's going on with him?"

"Legally speaking, I—"

"I know I'm not family. I get that. And I know that none of them out there are, either. But they are the closest thing he has."

I wait, but she still seems hesitant. I understand. She has already gone above and beyond and done some things that could threaten her career. She needs to be careful. But maybe I can help with that.

"Can you at least confirm to me that they are significantly similar symptoms to the other two, and that you would consider him to be in serious condition?"

She doesn't say a word, but she gives me a look. And that's all I need.

CHAPTER TWENTY-SIX

"Is Bellamy alright?"

"Not exactly," I say. "She's holding up, but she's really upset."

"I should be there with her."

"Eric, you were just released from the hospital yesterday. You can't be here and she understands that. She misses you, too, and she is looking forward to getting home to you and the baby. I'm not trying to be insensitive here, but since I've already been informed that I tend to do that when I'm trying to get something done, I might as well just lean fully into it. I need your authorization on this one."

"Why is it that you aren't in my position?" he asks. "I get nearly beaten to death and they still have me as interim supervisor. Why didn't they just go on and put you in Creagan's place?"

"Because he tried to frame me for murder. A couple times. And I shot a guy in the face not too long ago and he fell off a cliff."

"That was self-defense. You weren't even brought up on charges."

"Still worth noting," I counter. "But unless something changes sometime soon, it's looking like Interim Supervisor is just turning into Supervisor. And right now, I need my supervisor to authorize me turning this into an official Bureau investigation. There are two dead victims and one man is in very serious condition. The doctor was able to stabilize him when he arrived at the hospital, but he hasn't been recovering and has been put in a medically induced coma to help his body heal. They are hopeful, but there is the chance he won't survive. This could be a serial killer in the making."

"I thought you said one of those victims killed himself," Eric says.

"That's what we first thought, and it still hasn't been proven or disproven. That's the problem. We need to find out what happened. Darren doesn't have any family, which means no next of kin. The doctors won't discuss his condition and we can't access records, toxicology, or anything unless there is an official investigation. The police department here is working on Liza and Finn, but they don't have much to go on."

"Are they agreeable to us getting involved?" Eric asks.

"Yes. I've already spoken to the two detectives who have been involved in the investigation so far and told them the new development with Darren. They are not only willing to have us participate in the investigation, they appreciate the offer and think it would be beneficial for me to head it up."

"You sure you want to take that on?" he asks.

"What do you mean?"

"I just want to make sure this is something you want to do," he clarifies. "I know you already have a lot going on."

"Have you ever known me to purposely turn down a case I believe in because of other things I'm doing?" I ask.

"No, but with the holidays and your anniversary and everything coming up, I didn't know if you would want something else. And according to what Bellamy was telling me, this one might be tough," he says.

"So, I work harder. What's going on, Eric?" I ask.

"Nothing," he says quickly. Too quickly. It's that burst of response that comes when someone is trying too hard to be convincing. He hesitates before continuing. "I don't know how much more Bellamy can take."

The admission is hard for him. I know he hates feeling so helpless when it comes to her. He wants to protect her, to be able to do anything in his power to make things easier for her. This is indescribably difficult for her and he can't even be with her. I can understand why he would worry about her turning this into a full investigation and having her right in the middle of it.

But that can't stop us. Sometimes it's the hardest situations, the most difficult and painful to face, that are the most important ones to rush into headlong. In a way, it's a saving grace that Bellamy isn't a field agent. That means she won't have to delve as deep. She won't have to see or think the things I do. She'll know what I find out, but the separation will go a far way in protecting her.

At the same time, the fact that she won't be an active part of the investigation could frustrate her. She'll want to put herself in it and try to be the voice of the friends she's lost. But I can't let that happen. They deserve to speak, but they'll have to speak for themselves. They have to be the ones to tell their own story to me, rather than having it come through the filter of Bellamy.

Even if that means all I have to listen to is their tissues and bones.

"I know this is hard for her," I tell him. "But it won't be any easier pretending it isn't happening or pushing it aside. She deserves to know the truth, just like the rest of them do."

"You're right," he says. "I'm sorry. I just hate feeling like there's nothing that I can do."

"You just focus on getting better and taking care of Bebe. Hold down the Emperor investigation and stay sharp about Jonah. I'll handle things here."

"Have you heard anything more from him?" he asks.

"Not in a few days. He's gone quiet, which is rarely a good thing. But hopefully, it's just that he doesn't have anything interesting or disturbing to say. I know he's doing his own informal investigation into Miley and the Emperor killings, which isn't necessarily a good thing. Just keep your ears open and your eye out so you can notice anything that might track him down. Eventually, we'll draw him out."

"You will," Eric encourages me. "It's not going to be anyone else. It's going to be you."

"Because it's my fault he is the way he is?" I ask.

It's the first time I've really acknowledged what he said to me other than simply not speaking to him, and Eric goes silent.

"Emma, I'm sorry I said that," he sighs. "It was stupid and it isn't true."

"That's the thing though, Eric. It is true. And that's why it got me as much as it did. I just need to know that you know I'll never let who he is stop me from doing my job the best I can. Just carrying on a conversation with him as if I'm not doing everything I possibly can to hunt him down is one of the hardest things I've ever had to do. But I know in the end I'm doing the right thing."

"You are," he agrees. "You're doing what you need to so that one day he'll be back where he's supposed to be and you still get answers for the people he hurt."

"He's going to keep hurting them, Eric."

"I know."

"I have to stop him."

"I know that, too."

"But for now…"

"You need to do this. And you have my full approval. This is now a Bureau investigation."

When I get back to the hospital, Regan is pacing back and forth up the hallway and Priscilla has curled into herself again, sitting on a chair and staring down at her knees. She's either in prayer or just hoping that no one is going to look at her so she doesn't have to take part in the conversation.

"What happened?" Bellamy asks as she comes around the corner and sees me.

She's carrying a large cardboard container of coffee in each hand and has a plastic bag from the hospital cafeteria dangling from her arm. If I know Bellamy, no one asked her to go get anything. She did because she needed to move and feel like she was doing something useful rather than just standing around waiting.

"Where are Maya and Adam?" I ask.

The three of them shake their heads, but seconds later, the pair come from the opposite direction. Maya has her hand wrapped around his arm and is leaned toward him like he's supporting her, but I can't help but notice Adam's eyes focused stiffly ahead.

"Where were you?" Regan asks.

"I went down to the chapel," Maya explains. "I needed some time to think and reflect. Send up a prayer for Darren." She lets out a shuddering sob. "While I was on my way down there, I ran into Adam, so he came with me."

"Emma just got back," Bellamy tells her.

Maya's eyes snap to me. "What did you find out?"

"Dr. Kelsey was very wary of giving any information for privacy reasons. The only way I could find out anything is through an official investigation," I state.

"The police are already investigating," Adam says.

"They are investigating Liza and Finn's deaths," I point out. "And officially it is still considered a murder-suicide. Like I told you, there usually has to be an investigation that shows some proof when situations like that occur. Very rarely is it just accepted that there was a murder and a suicide that happened at different times and have no other influences so there's no further investigation.

"But the extent of that investigation may very well be just looking for the true cause of death to show that it was, in fact, not a natural cause. Now that Darren is apparently experiencing the same symptoms, it makes the investigation more complicated and extensive."

"So, why don't you take over?" Regan asks.

"That's right," Maya adds. "You're FBI. You've solved crimes no one else was able to. If you don't think the police are going to do enough to look into this, why don't you just take over the investigation?"

"She can't," Priscilla tells them.

"What do you mean she can't?" Maya asks. "Of course, she can. She's an FBI agent. They are federal. She just needs to tell Detective Gabriel she's taking the case."

"Well, technically," I say, "Priscilla is right. The FBI is a separate entity from local law enforcement. I can't just bigfoot my way onto a crime scene. There are specifications that have to be met for it to be under FBI jurisdiction. Things like crimes that cross state lines, cyber crime, crimes involving the Post Office or postal employees. Or serial killers."

"Serial killers?" Bellamy asks softly, already knowing where I'm going with this.

"Anyway, I can't just force my way onto a case without specific approval from my superior. And I just got off the phone with him."

"Eric gave you approval," Bellamy whispers.

I nod. "This is now a Bureau investigation. Which means I can collect information about all three of them I might not have had access to before. But that doesn't mean I can just share that information with you. It's a federal investigation and that means there are details I can't share with the public. Since he has no family, there is no next of kin to discuss information with and he couldn't provide a release for HIPAA. The doctor may refuse to provide any information to any of you, but she may also request you choose one representative."

"Which of us would be the representative?" Priscilla asks.

Adam looks like he is going to volunteer, but Maya steps forward. "It should be me."

"Why?" Bellamy asks.

Maya takes a deep breath. "Darren and I have been seeing each other."

CHAPTER TWENTY-SEVEN

BELLAMY SHAKES HER HEAD, HER ARMS CROSSED TIGHTLY OVER her chest as she stares down the hallway toward Darren's room.

"I just don't understand. They didn't tell any of us that they were seeing each other," she says.

"Maya said it was new," I shrug. "And that because of everything that's been going on, they decided they didn't want to make a big deal out of it. They didn't want it to seem like they were trying to take attention away from Liza and Finn's deaths."

"But there was nothing," Priscilla says. "Even when the whole group was together, they didn't pay any particular attention to each other."

"Maybe that was on purpose," Regan offers. "If they wanted to kind of keep things under the radar, they wouldn't spend a lot of time showing affection to each other."

"But she's been leaning on Adam more than anything."

"We've known each other a long time," Adam is quick to point out. "We knew each other before we met the rest of you."

I didn't know that. It's a small detail and might not mean anything at all, but it's something. I tuck it away in the back of my mind to think about later.

"We can figure out the particulars later, I announce. "What matters right now is that she can be with him. She can keep an eye on him and give the rest of you details about how he's doing. Just dating him or being his girlfriend doesn't make her his next of kin, so the medical team isn't going to defer to her for any decisions or anything. They will continue to be fully in the lead for all decisions regarding treatment, testing, everything."

That stops the swarm of bickering and everyone nods at me.

"I'm going to go talk to Dr. Kelsey again and see what I can find out. I need to let her know this is an official investigation and ask her to start taking observations that might be useful for Darren and for finding out what happened to the others. I think the rest of you should take a break."

"What do you mean?" Regan asks.

"It's not going to do any of you any good to just hang out around here. I promise you I will make sure you get all relevant information as it comes up. Anything I'm allowed to share, I will. But for now, you need to take care of yourselves, too, and you're not going to be able to do that sitting at the hospital," I tell them.

"She's right," Bellamy says. "Besides, as much as none of us want to think about it, we really should get in touch with Liza and Finn's families. They reached out right after Liza's death and said they'd be coming into town, but I haven't heard anything from them since. We should talk to them about how they want to handle everything. Now that Finn isn't going to be able to handle Liza's interment, it's up to her family to decide what to do. And his family needs to manage his final wishes."

I hug Bellamy and notice a different smell than her usual perfume. She's worn the same scent for years, so it's strange for it to be different now.

"You smell different," I say. "It's nice. Just different."

She nods. "I ran out of my perfume. This is one of Maya's scents."

She and the others head out of the hospital and I make my way to Dr. Kelsey's office. She is with a patient, so I take out my phone while I wait. I missed a call from Sam, and seeing his name on the screen makes my heart both happy and heavy. I hate that I've missed so many calls and messages from him recently. I hope he knows he really is my priority. I don't ever want him to think that I'm ignoring him or that I don't love him with every ounce of my being every moment of every day.

I should probably take as many opportunities as I can to tell him that. I think I do, but there's always time for more. There's a lot of time to make up for. Too many years that I didn't tell him and thought I would never get the chance.

"I love you," I say as soon as he answers my call back. "And I miss you. And I am so grateful for your support and that I found my way to you again."

"Thank you, babe," he says. "I love and miss you, and I'm so grateful for you, too. Is there something going on? Are you safe?"

It's a valid question. I probably should have considered how it would sound for him to hear me say things like that when he knows I'm knee-deep in serial killers at this particular juncture in my career.

"Yes," I tell him. "Sorry. I'm fine. I just wanted to tell you that. I saw I'd missed your call and it upset me. I wanted to make sure you knew I wasn't ignoring you or just not answering your calls because something was more important."

"Would you even be you if you weren't the busiest woman on the planet?" he jokes. "I knew what I signed up for when I said 'I do.'"

"Yeah, well I'm even busier now," I say. "I'm officially investigating on behalf of the Bureau."

"That's good," Sam says. "You'll be able to figure it out."

"Thank you," I say, letting out a breath. "How are things going with you? Anything else from the dealer?"

"Nothing beneficial," he says. "He insists he doesn't know Marie and never has. And when she disappeared, he was already in prison."

"Jonah was in prison for a lot of his crimes," I point out.

"Yeah, but this guy is no Jonah. I'm still trying to track her movements in the last few days that people heard from her. There are some calls and things, but I don't want to rely on those. I'm specifically looking for people who actually saw her so I have a concrete timeline. I just need to figure out where she went," he says.

We talk for a little longer before the door opens and Dr. Kelsey comes in. I get off the phone with Sam and wave my phone at her slightly before putting it away.

"My husband," I explain.

She nods as she sits down beside me. "He stayed home?"

"Actually, he's in Michigan. His cousin has been missing, so he went to help with the search," I say.

Her eyebrows raise slightly. "A lot going on in both of your lives."

"Always," I nod. "I think that's inevitable when you combine the FBI and a Sheriff's department."

"Do you manage it alright?" she asks. She immediately looks uncomfortable. "I'm sorry. That was invasive."

"No," I shake my head. "It's alright. I'd probably ask the same thing if I wasn't one of us." I laugh slightly. "I'm not going to say it's easy. A lot of the time it's really not. But we understand each other and we're supportive of our careers. We both know that if our careers ever really got in the way of our marriage and started causing problems for either of us, we would choose each other first. We've known each other since we were really young and a lot of people have told us they always thought we were supposed to be together."

"So, you dated before?" she asks.

I nod. "When we were teenagers. At that time in my life, I was sure he was it for me. I didn't have a doubt in my mind I was going to go to college, graduate, marry him, and everything was going to be perfect."

"Nothing ever really works out like that when we're young, does it?" she asks. "Life sort of gets in the way."

"Well, not exactly," I explain. "I broke up with him because I decided to go into the Bureau. I felt like I couldn't focus on that career and be married to him at the same time. But I needed to choose the FBI. My father had just disappeared and I couldn't take losing anyone else."

She nods. "Your father's story is a pretty incredible one."

"It is."

There's a slight pause before she shakes her head, her eyes closing briefly like she's attempting to reset the thoughts going through her mind.

"I'm sorry. We went off the rails a little. I think my brain just needed a bit of a detour."

"That's alright," I smile. "I can understand that. I wanted to talk about Darren more. Now that I'm officially investigating this situation, I need as much information as I can possibly get."

She runs down all of the symptoms Darren had when he first arrived at the hospital and the ones he continues to exhibit. They've been keeping him under since they stabilized him and have seen a slight improvement, but there's still a lot of questions to answer.

"It's definitely suspicious," she says. "Not only is it strange for them all to have the same symptoms, but for it to happen on this timeline, when they weren't near each other. It's very suspicious."

"It is very odd. We know that Liza was having an affair, but there was nothing in the journals to indicate who she was having it with. Now I have to consider whether it might be Darren. It doesn't eliminate my original theory that Finn murdered his wife and then killed himself. It just means he managed to find a way to attempt to murder Darren from beyond the grave."

"But how?" she wonders.

"That's the big question. He obviously would have had to have started the process before his own death. But why didn't it work?

And was that part of why he killed himself? We know that Finn was at Darren's house the night before he was found dead. The question is, what did he do while he was there?"

"I'm doing my best to help you find out," she says.

"I know you are," I say. "But I think there's one more thing we need to do."

"What's that?" she asks.

"I think there needs to be a camera in Darren's room."

"I'll get it done," she says.

CHAPTER TWENTY-EIGHT

Detective Gabriel meets me at the police department an hour later. He sits down with me in a conference room, a file of all the information from the cases sitting between us.

"I have everything that we've found compiled in here," he says.

"Thank you," I tell him, taking the folder and looking into it. "What about other cases? Have there been any other deaths with similar circumstances any time recently?"

"Yes, actually," he nods. "Not exactly the same, but there are similarities. A few weeks ago, a woman named Cheryl Bishop was found dead in her house. She was in bed and there were signs in the house she had experienced vomiting leading up to her death."

"Who found her?"

"A neighbor," he explains. "There was a really intense storm the night before and apparently there was some damage to her yard and part of her house. They wanted to make sure she was alright, but they didn't know her phone number. Cheryl's car was in place, but she didn't answer when the neighbor knocked on the door."

"What did the death investigation show?" I ask.

"There wasn't a ton of information available since she lived alone and didn't really socialize with her neighbors. It made it a little tougher to really piece events together. But from what they could gather from the evidence immediately obvious in the house was that she was getting ready for bed when the storm started. There was water in the tub and a damp towel. Some dishes showed she had been eating as well.

"At some point, she started feeling sick and vomited in the bathroom. There were a couple of bottles of bath products on the floor, so it looked like she either went into the bathroom in the dark after the electricity went out, or she was disoriented and off-balance and knocked them over. She then went into her bedroom, where she died," he says.

"Was there an autopsy?"

"Yes," he nods. "No sign of drugs or poison. No unusual tox reports. There was no sign of violence on her body. Essentially we have no idea what happened."

"Okay. Can I get the file for that case, too? Just so I can look over it?"

"You got it."

"I appreciate it."

That night at the hotel, I look through the case file for Cheryl Bishop, comparing the details of her death to Liza, Finn, and Darren. There are some very obvious similarities, but then also details that don't correspond at all. The toxicology report doesn't show anything unusual, just like the detective told me. No sign of any type of controlled substance or any of the usual toxins or contaminants they test for. In essence, they had no idea what happened to her. She, like the others, seemed like a perfectly healthy woman who ended up dead for seemingly no reason.

The next morning, I'm getting ready to go to the hospital when my phone rings. It's Detective Gabriel. I hold up a finger to Bellamy to ask her to wait for a second while I talk to him.

"You coming in to talk to me must have been good luck yesterday," he starts.

"Why do you say that?" I ask.

"Because we've been waiting for reports from the toxicology for Liza Fielding and tests from materials throughout her house. We just got some reports back this morning," he tells me.

"The toxicology?" I ask.

"Yes," he says. "That can take quite a while."

"I'm well aware," I say. "At this point, I was just hoping up for a bit of an early Christmas miracle."

"Well, I can't offer you that. But I can tell you that several materials from throughout the Fielding home were tested after Finn Fielding's death. The department tested all open food and drink products, open containers in the refrigerator, and dishes that were in the sink and in the dishwasher to find traces of any contaminants or poisons," he says.

"And did they find anything?" I ask.

"You could say that," he says. "In the salt shaker."

"What was it?" I ask.

"Arsenic."

⁂

"That's amazing," Xavier says over video chat a few minutes after I get off the phone with the detective.

"Maybe not so loud," I say. "Bellamy is really upset about this news. We were going to go to the hospital, but I told her I thought it would be best if she took a break. She hasn't been sleeping well or eating well, so I have her in a bath right now and I'm going to try to get her to rest this afternoon."

"That's a good idea," Dean says. "Are you going to go talk to the doctor?"

"I'm going to have to later," I say. "She needs to know exactly what she's working with. It might help her save Darren."

"That explains the symptoms," Xavier nods. But he doesn't look convinced or like he feels confident in the finding.

"What is it, Xavier?" I ask. "It looks like you're thinking about something."

"I'm always thinking about something," he counters.

"This is true," I admit. "But you look like you're thinking about something specific."

"I told you that this sounded like arsenic," he says. "The symptoms sound right, and while it's not something you can just pick up at the grocery store like you used to be able to, it isn't impossible to find."

"So why don't you seem like you think it's what happened anymore?"

"It's just the idea of possibly poisoning himself with arsenic. It's an extremely effective form of murder, and by extension, suicide. And it's not completely unheard of for somebody to take arsenic to themselves as a way of heading out of this world on their own terms. But it's extremely unusual. Death by arsenic is extremely unpleasant and painful. Arsenic-ing yourself doesn't seem like a great way to go. Not to mention it's not exactly quick," he says.

"But it has been," I point out. "They've been developing symptoms and dying within just a few hours."

"Which is unusual," Xavier replies. "Arsenic is extremely lethal and can cause death within a very short time if given in massive doses. But that is extremely rare. Somebody taking a large enough dose of arsenic to be fatal would very likely detect the taste of the poison in whatever they were consuming and stop consuming it. And even if they did get it all the way in, the probable scenario is that their body would reject it. Not enough would stay in the bloodstream to cause death that fast.

"It's not impossible. Just unlikely. For the most part, arsenic is a long-term poisoning situation. Unlike other poisons, it doesn't break down and get fully processed out of the body. It builds up. Very tiny amounts can be given over an extended period so that the toxicity level builds up until it becomes fatal."

"The poison was found in the salt shaker," I say. "If Finn put it there to poison Liza, why would he also be consuming it himself over that time?"

"Beats me."

"Could it be that somebody else poisoned their salt shaker to kill them?" Dean ponders.

"That would be unusual," I note. "Seems like a pretty dicey way of trying to murder someone."

"Well, we're no strangers to the unusual anymore," Xavier comments.

"You can say that again," Dean tells him.

"We're no strangers to—"

"Xavier, it was a figure of speech."

I'm still thinking about the conversation with Xavier a couple of hours later when Bellamy wakes up from the nap she finally managed to fall into. She sits up and pulls the blankets up around her.

"How do you feel?" I ask.

She shrugs. "Kind of numb. Like I've run out of the amount of sadness and grief I can feel."

"I know how that is," I say. "It's not a horrible thing. Savor it for a little while."

She nods. "I know this is all going to really hit me at some point. I just don't know what I'm going to do. I can't believe they're gone."

"I know," I say. "I'm so sorry you're going through this." I hesitate for a second, feeling inappropriate and awkward about the question I'm about to ask, but I know it's important. "B, can you tell me more about them?"

"What do you mean?" she asks. "What do you want to know?"

"Anything you can tell me. Just tell me about them. Anything I can find out that might give me more insight into who they were, their relationships, their lifestyles. It might help me identify something that didn't stand out before."

She nods and reaches onto the table beside her for a bottle of water, taking a sip and letting it rest in her mouth for a second before swallowing it.

"I think the other day Adam mentioned that he and Maya met first. They actually grew up near each other and went to high school together. They dated for a really short while, then went their separate ways. It was just a couple of months later when they went to college and ended up in the class together, so they rekindled their friendship."

"They were together?" I ask.

"I wouldn't really say they were together. They just went out a couple of times. In college, they seemed like they might get a second chance. They were a bit flirty for a while and I want to say they went out on like one or two dates, but nothing came of it."

"It seems like Maya is very reliant on him," I say.

She nods. "She always has leaned on him. They were pretty close and still are, so I think she feels comfortable with him."

"What about the rest of the group?" I ask. "Were there any other pairings? Anybody else who tried to date each other?"

"Well, you heard that Maya's apparently dating Darren now? That was kind of a surprise. He actually introduced Priscilla to the rest of the group because he had a crush on her. She had no idea at the time that he felt that way and thought he was just a nice guy from her study group. He did end up telling her years later and they thought it was really funny, but nothing came of it. Finn and Liza were the old married couple. They'd been together for so long. But she used to tease him that he had a crush on Regan at one point."

"This seems really complicated," I say.

"It's like an episode of a bad old nineties sitcom, is what it is," Bellamy grouses. "I never got wrapped up in any of that. The guys were strictly friends for me. Nothing else."

"That's probably a good philosophy in a situation like that," I say.

"How about careers? What does everybody do? I know you mentioned Liza was a lawyer. What about everybody else?"

I listen as Bellamy tells me all about the group of friends as they went through college and moved on to their careers. She tells me about how Liza's law office had recently joined Maya on a creative venture. Finn jumped around a bit but settled on a corporate job. Regan works in advertising. Adam is a contractor and owns an extremely successful firm. Maya started out as a nurse but recently started a business with Liza creating gift baskets and other experiences. Priscilla lives on a trust fund given to her by her extraordinarily wealthy grandfather and occasionally works in things that amuse her, like giving tours at local historic sites.

She tells me stories about them, drifting back and forth between giving me the details and facts that I need and offering me glimpses into their friendships and how they developed. Nothing immediately jumps out at me, but I feel like I know them better and that is meaningful.

When she finished, I decide I have to tell her the truth. As gently as I can, I let her know about the arsenic in the saltshaker. She takes it better than I expect. It obviously affects her, but she remains calm, simply saying we need to get to the hospital and check on him.

CHAPTER TWENTY-NINE

I STILL DON'T THINK IT'S USEFUL FOR THE FRIENDS TO HOVER AROUND the hospital all the time, just waiting for something to happen. It seems they've taken my advice for the most part. A couple of them have drifted in and out, but they aren't staying for long anymore.

The only one who is staying around all day is Maya. She's dedicated to being there for Darren and taking care of him. There isn't much she can do, though. Doctor Kelsey already made a note that no food or drinks were to be given to Darren even when he woke up without her prior approval. Because he's still unconscious, he only receives what can go into his system through the machines hooked up to him.

But she stays anyway. She stays beside his bed and works on her computer or beads. Sometimes she even reads to him. Every day she carefully applies lotion to his skin to keep it from drying out and lip balm to his lips to prevent them from getting chapped. She brushes his hair and occasionally taps into her nurse's training to move his arms and legs around a little bit.

I wonder if it's more difficult for her and others in the medical field to see somebody they care about going through such a difficult thing and not being able to do anything about it. She might not be a nurse anymore, but that's in her. That type of training and education doesn't just go away. And neither does the commitment and love of it. Sometimes nurses get disenfranchised or lose their passion because of things that they experience, but for the most part, anyone who has ever been a nurse or a doctor maintains that sense of responsibility and nurturing.

She hasn't spoken much since the first day she was allowed to go in. I was hoping we would get more information from her being in there, but she keeps everything close to her chest. I know she wishes there was something more she could do, but we are all at a loss.

She comes out of Darren's room and seems to be heading for the coffee machine when she notices me. She comes towards me a few steps and smiles softly.

"Hi, Emma," she says. "Good to see you."

She's definitely more subdued, but I understand that.

"How are you holding up?" I ask. "You're leaving, right? You're not trying to stay here all the time?"

"They won't let me," she sighs. "Since we aren't married, I'm not allowed to stay over. I'm technically supposed to only be here during visitation hours, but I've managed to add some wiggle room to that."

"That's good to hear," I say. "You need to take care of yourself, too. You can't just pour everything into somebody else and not expect to crash and burn because of it."

"You don't have to warn me about that," she says. "I am well versed in stress and pushing myself too hard."

"I'm sorry," I say.

She stares at me for a second, then shakes her head and sighs. "You don't need to apologize. I shouldn't be taking this out on you. And I shouldn't have before. The only reason we know anything at all is because of how much you've done for us. Thank you."

I nod. "Of course."

"I want us to get together this weekend. Regan's family owns an incredible lake house near here and I am going to ask her if we can spend the weekend together having some amazing food, spending time together, and memorializing our friends. A special Friendsgiving."

"That sounds... lovely," I say, not really meaning it, but not knowing what else to say.

The word "Friendsgiving" is completely out of place in the midst of the situation we're in. It stands out awkwardly, like a Fun Run in the middle of the Easter festivities at a Southern Baptist church. I can understand the compulsion to want to get together, but the wording of it makes me a little squeamish.

"I'm glad to hear you say that," Maya says. "Because I want you to come."

"Me?"

"Of course. We wouldn't be anywhere with finding out what happened to people we love if it wasn't for you. I know you haven't been around for a long time the way we have, but you are a part of us now and I want you to be there. Please say you'll come."

It's not like I can say no. I said before this case feels like a game of *Clue*. Now I'm agreeing to go lock myself in the mansion.

"I'll come," I say. "Bellamy and I will come together."

"That's amazing. I'm really looking forward to it. I think it will be good for all of us."

∽

"This says that the medical examiner suspected poisoning because of the symptoms and the quick onset of death, so a far more thorough toxicology test was run to look for things that aren't usually looked for in one," I say.

I'm flipping through pictures of Cheryl Bishop's house.

"I didn't realize that wasn't something that would automatically be looked for," Bellamy says. "I guess I just assumed if they were testing a person who was dead, they would look for everything."

"That's what most people think," I tell her. "There's a common misconception that samples are put through some sort of process and a computer just spits out everything present in the body. Like it can draw it out automatically. In reality, every compound has to be searched for specifically. The standard toxicology looks for things like alcohol, antidepressants, cardiovascular drugs, painkillers, antipsychotics, cocaine, other narcotics. The most basic things. None of those showed up for Cheryl."

"Did they have any idea of how long it's going to take for Liza and Finn?" Bellamy asks.

"They are putting a rush on it, but it could still take a couple more days. Dr. Kelsey also sent additional samples to be specifically tested for arsenic. It was found in the house in the saltshaker, but nowhere near Darren."

I go through the pictures again. Something is standing out to me, but I can't put my finger on it. No matter how many times I look at the images, I can't figure out exactly what's standing out to me.

"What do you think happened to him?" Bellamy asks. "Do you still think Finn could have killed himself and the others? Even with the delayed reaction from Darren?"

"Right now, I don't have a fully-formed idea. But I don't think that's impossible. Maya and Darren are a couple right now, but do you think there's any chance he could have been the one having an affair with Liza?"

"Darren?" She raises both eyebrows. "I don't think so. I really don't."

"Why not?" I ask.

"They just don't seem to mesh in that way. It's not that they don't like each other, because they do. It's just that in the greater context of the group, they have always been two who seem to really depend on at least two or three of the others to be around them when they spent time together. I know he and Maya have been doing a good job of keeping things on the down-low, but Darren just doesn't have it in him to keep two relationships like that totally silent."

My phone chimes and I pick it up to check the text waiting for me.

"It's Xavier," I tell her. "He wants to know if I'll make him a chocolate silk pie for dessert for Thanksgiving."

Bellamy sighs. "I can't believe that's so close."

"I know," I say. "It doesn't really feel like it anymore. Sam is coming home in time for it, and I can't wait. But it does feel different."

"You're still doing it, aren't you? At your house?"

"Like always. As long as I am physically able, I will prepare that meal. Speaking of which, though, how do you feel about this weekend at Regan's lake house?"

"I think it's a sweet idea," she says. "Not something I necessarily would have thought about. Thinking about having a Friendsgiving when your friends are dying, doesn't exactly mesh for me. But I talked to Regan about it, and she's pumped. Priscilla said it was a really nice thought, too."

I nod. I'm outnumbered. It seems I'm definitely going.

CHAPTER THIRTY

Maya wasn't exaggerating. The lake house is absolutely gorgeous. It sits at the end of a long driveway lined with oaks glowing in their autumn gold and orange and rises up into the sky that's such a shade of dusty blue it looks like the rippling water of the lake itself. As for the water, it's a matter of feet from the back of the house. A massive multi-level deck extends out of the back of the house and feeds onto a long dock that extends out across the back lawn and out far into the lake. There, it spreads again into a floating dock that I'm sure has hosted dozens of excellent parties.

If it wasn't for the circumstances, I would probably be thrilled to be somewhere like this. It's beautiful and I've always been drawn to the water. I'm not a big swimmer. Not that I won't swim, that's just not the primary draw of the water to me. So the fact that it's late November and far too chilly to take a dip doesn't bother me. If I was here for my own vacation with my friends, I could see myself bringing a thick blanket out to that floating deck and curling up in it for long afternoons of reading.

Bellamy and I seem to be the last to arrive. The others are already gathered inside, sitting in a formal parlor off to the side of the front door. Trays with snacks, coffee, and tea sit on several different surfaces throughout the room. I try hard not to draw comparisons between this and the memorial for Liza at the sorority house.

Regan smiles when we walk into the house. "Welcome."

"This place is beautiful," I marvel.

"Thank you. My family has owned it for generations. We do family reunions and weddings and things here," she tells me.

"I can see why."

"Come on in," she gestures me in. "I'll show you to your rooms and then you can come back and have some snacks. I'm sure you're hungry after your drive."

I have to admit, I've never really understood that statement. There's nothing inherent about driving that should make you hungry afterward. I suppose not everyone is like me, who insists on having snacks within arm's reach at all times, but even then, the lake house is only a half an hour drive outside of town. That hardly warrants a restorative meal afterward.

But we thank her and allow her to bring us up a sprawling set of stairs to the third floor of the house. She directs us to rooms down the hall from one another. Inside, the room is done up to look woodsy and casual, but the luxury linens and fine furniture give away its true personality. It's bigger than Bellamy's first apartment, and again I can see myself really enjoying a relaxing vacation somewhere like this.

I put down my luggage and walk around, looking at all the details. I notice a basket sitting on the dresser filled with body products and scented candles along with a pair of socks and a sleeping mask. It reminds me of some of the welcome baskets from high-end resorts I've stayed in—mostly while on undercover assignments.

I pick up a container of lotion and take off the lid to smell it. It's a sweet vanilla base with warm, spicy undertones.

"Do you like it?" The sudden question behind me makes me jump slightly and I whip around to see Maya standing in the doorway. "I'm sorry. I didn't mean to startle you."

"It's alright. I didn't hear you come up."

She comes further into the room, pointing at the lotion in my hands. "I just wanted to tell you about that. It's from the company I owned with Liza. We dreamed of making gift baskets for people with the products and candles we make. It started out really small with just people we knew, but it was getting really popular."

"This is a really wonderful smell." I look at the label. " Vanilla Bourbon Black Pepper Sugar. I guess you decided not to go with any of those whimsical names some people put on soap and things."

Maya lets out a soft laugh and shakes her head. "No. Liza didn't want to do that. She said it was much more sophisticated to just put what the smells are right on the bottle. High-end clients aren't looking for kitschy names. They want a luxurious smell. That one is actually one of Liza's. She loved it. She said it was perfect for everybody."

I nod. "I can see that. It could definitely work for either men or women, and a range of ages." I take out some of the lotion and rub it into my hands. It's thick, smooth, and feels creamy and deeply hydrating in my skin. As I breathe in another lungful of the scent, I realize it's the same scent that Bellamy was wearing the other day when she hugged me. "There's a hint of something else in the background. What is that?"

"A secret," Maya winks. Then she smiles and shakes her head. "It's tobacco. A lot of people don't realize that's a pretty popular fragrance profile, especially for men's colognes. It's spicy and deep, and can skew sweet depending on what it is paired with. I love it with vanilla, so when I first smelled this blend, I knew it was going to be really popular. And I was right. It's one of our best sellers." She looks around and lets out a nostalgic, somewhat sad sigh. "Anyway, I'll leave you to settle in a bit. I just wanted to check on you because you've never been here before. Is there anything you need?"

I shake my head. "No. I'll be down in just a bit."

"Okay. Well, if you do think of anything, don't hesitate to let us know. We're really glad you're here."

She leaves and I wait a few seconds before walking out of my room and down to Bellamy's. She is carefully unpacking her suitcase and putting items away in the dresser. She has the same basket sitting on a side table and I walk over to it. It has the same fragrance, but I notice an extra small bottle tucked into the front. I pick it up to see that it's bubble bath in the same scent as the rest of the products. I didn't notice one in my basket. Maybe I will ask Maya for some. A bubble bath sounds amazing.

When Bellamy is ready, we go downstairs and Regan gives me the tour of the house. I can imagine the friends getting together here as often as possible. And when she shows me the kitchen, I see a couple of the little crates Darren uses to pack his coffee. I remember what they said about him making a blend for each of his friends. That brings a sad smile to my lips. I hope he can pull through.

CHAPTER THIRTY-ONE

THE FIRST EVENING TOGETHER IS PLEASANT, IF A LITTLE SAD AND strained. There seems to be a constant stream of food available and I find myself hesitant to eat any of it, but the others delve in without concern. Almost as if she can sense what I'm thinking, Regan casually offers that she was so lucky to be able to arrange for grocery delivery just this morning. Usually this close to Thanksgiving it's much harder to get groceries to the house.

I feel like it's her way of telling me all the food is fresh and safe. After dinner, Priscilla suggests we go outside and start a fire in the backyard fire pit. It was always one of Liza's favorite things to do here, so it feels appropriate to start off the tributes to them.

We gather the supplies for a fire along with coffee and add marshmallows to roast. When I step out onto the back deck, I realize just how chilly it is from the wind blowing in off the water. I step back inside and hurry to my room to grab one of the thick sweaters I brought along.

The marshmallows make me think of Xavier, and I'm thinking about a special treat I can bring to him when I walk out of my room and turn down the hallway.

I'd been distracted by putting on my sweater and trying to decide if Xavier would prefer a gourmet marshmallow or gourmet chocolate to put on his marshmallow, and I'm partway down the hallway before I realize I made a wrong turn. Rather than going all the way to the end of the hall and turning to make my way to the steps and back down, I turned only halfway down the hall. It brings me further into the wing of bedrooms.

Before I can turn back around, I hear voices. They are muffled but don't sound like they're coming from one of the rooms. Curiosity makes me pause. One of the voices is definitely a woman and she sounds less than happy.

I get a little closer and recognize the voice as Maya.

"I just don't understand why you're acting like this. You know what we have. We've always had."

"No, I don't, Maya. You have to stop this."

It's Adam's voice. He sounds frustrated and exasperated.

"How can you say that?"

"Maya, we are here this weekend to remember our friends who are dead. I seriously can't believe you're doing this right now," he says.

"I'm doing it because of them. This just shows how short life is. Anything can happen at any second. None of us expected Liza or Finn to die. Or for Darren to be in the hospital. We all had all kinds of plans with both of them. We just figured they were going to be around forever. And now look. We could lose all three of them and have to go to the rest of our lives wondering what could have happened if they were still with us. I don't want to do that with you."

"I know what could happen if we spend our lives together. It's exactly what I've always wanted to happen. I love you and I know you still love me. I know it probably feels awkward because of my relationship with Darren and everything, but we can't keep living our lives for other people. We need to do what's right for us, and that's to be together. Officially. Out in the open."

"Maya, you need to stop. I'm not talking about this."

Feeling just the slightest bit guilty about standing there and listening to their conversation, I turn and hurry down the hall so that I'll be downstairs by the time they join us. Bellamy looks at me with raised eyebrows as I come outside.

"Everything okay?"

I nod, not sure if I should tell her about the conversation I just heard. I remember what she told me about their complicated history, and I can't help but wonder just how many other secrets this group has. They seem to know each other so well, and yet every time we turn around, something else comes to the surface that shakes that sense of unity.

Out at the firepit, we toast marshmallows and the conversation turns again to sharing memories of Liza and Finn. A few of Darren seep in, each time shifting the feeling a bit more somber. It's not a fun thought that he might not ever make it out of that hospital room. He's been doing better, but not enough that his body is really recovering. He's still being kept under.

After a couple of marshmallows, I walk over to the deep wooden tray where a French press of hot coffee waits alongside a pitcher of cream and a bowl of coarse raw sugar. Filling a mug with just pure black coffee, I go back to sit beside Bellamy on one of the benches made of rough-hewn logs.

"Tomorrow I think we should have a real memorial for Liza and Finn," Regan suggests.

"And a vigil for Darren," Maya adds.

"That would be beautiful. We could do it right out on the dock. They all love the water," Priscilla says.

"That's perfect," Maya smiles. "Adam, you should say a few words. You've always been the most eloquent one of all of us. You're so good with words. You can make anyone feel anything."

He looks at her for a brief second, then nods. "I could do that."

To my side, I notice Bellamy is curled over, her hands pressed between her knees as she rocks slightly. I reach over and touch her back, making her lean to the side toward me.

"Are you alright?" I whisper.

"I just…" she looks around at her friends. "I just need a second."

She stands, balls the blanket she had draped around her into her arms, and rushes up the dock toward the house. Maya starts to move toward her, but I stand first.

"I've got her," I tell her. "I think we'll probably turn in. It's getting pretty late. We'll see everyone in the morning. Goodnight."

I run after Bellamy and find her in her room, sitting in the middle of the bed, crying.

"I'm sorry," she says as soon as I walk in.

"There's nothing for you to be sorry for."

"It just got to be too much for me," she says.

"It was getting to be too much for me and I barely even know them. I can't imagine what you're feeling right now. I wish there was something I could do to help you."

"You are, Emma," she says. "You're doing the most important thing. You're trying to find the truth."

"I just wish I knew where to look," I say. "The arsenic in the salt shaker makes sense for Liza and Finn. Maybe. I can see him putting it in the salt, feeding it to her, she dies, and he eats it himself. But that would be a really difficult death for him to put himself through."

"You know people do that sometimes, though. Once they make that decision to die, they don't always go with the method that seems like it would make the most sense. Some do. They go with a fast, easy option, but others, especially the ones who are killing themselves in response to hurting someone else, go for a punishment route. They want to feel pain and misery. If they can replicate what they did to their victim, so much the better," she says.

"Listen to you sounding like an investigator," I comment.

She smiles and gives a soft laugh, then starts to cry again.

"I just don't understand why. Why do this? If they were having trouble, they could have gone to a counselor or even just gotten divorced. Do people really think it's the end of the world if they admit they've made a mistake marrying someone, or just that their relationship has reached its end?" she asks.

"Some people do. They think that it makes them look like a failure and they can't face the embarrassment. I would think that would be especially difficult in a friend group like this. All of you know each other. You've known each other since before they were married. It would seem so strange to watch them go through a separation, and then to have to decide how you were going to navigate two separate friendships. Because even though people like to say they're going to stay friends, that very rarely happens. It would mean the group was fractured and people would have to choose loyalties and decide what to do with who. It's hard."

"Not hard enough to warrant killing somebody."

"I agree with you on that. Come on. Why don't you take a bubble bath and relax?"

Bellamy shakes her head. "I just want to go to sleep."

"Okay," I say. "I'll see you in the morning. But if you need me, I'm right down the hall."

"Goodnight."

"Night."

I go toward my room thinking about the conversation I overheard. Regardless of what was happening between the two of them, Adam was right to say this wasn't the time for Maya to be bringing it up. I can understand her feeling, wanting to grab onto life and cherish every second of it as they watch so many of their friends go through tragedy. I've been in that position myself more than I'd like to admit. But not now. Not when they are supposed to be memorializing those friends. She seems afraid, almost like she thinks it's going to happen again.

I can understand that, too. All around me, I can feel something like a timer counting down. Unless I can find out what happened and why, there's the chance it will happen again.

CHAPTER THIRTY-TWO

The next morning when I go down for breakfast, I encounter Priscilla coming into the house from outside. She's wearing leggings and a long-sleeve fleece shirt with an ear warmer around her head. Her cheeks are glowing bright red and her breath comes out of her lungs in big gulps. Cold air is always harder to breathe, and even though she looks like an experienced runner, it's hard to push through workouts like that in the winter.

I remember runs like that through temperatures far too low for me to be out. But they kept me feeling alive. They kept my body in the shape I needed to be the fiercest agent I could be. Even if it was sometimes hell doing it. And sometimes because it was hell. Going through that pain and forcing myself to go the full distance every day no matter what it was like disciplined me and made it so I was willing and able to overcome challenges many other agents do everything they can to avoid.

Priscilla smiles at me and reaches into her pocket.

"Good morning," she says.

"Morning. How was your run?"

"Cold," she admits. "But good." She pulls something out of her pocket and holds it out toward me. "I found this in my car right where I had the basket for your room when I was transporting them for Maya. It must have fallen out."

It's the missing bottle of bubble bath.

"Thank you," I smile. "I was actually looking forward to taking a bubble bath later."

"You should," she says. "Those products are incredible. I wish I could take one now, but they put me right to sleep."

I laugh. "Might be nice after the run."

She offers another small smile and I realize it's the most emotion I've seen from her the entire time I've known her. She seems more at peace out here.

"Definitely later. But I think it's just a shower for me this morning. Go on into the kitchen. There's always coffee and pastries in the morning."

"Do elves bring it?" I ask.

She gets closer to a laugh. "Sometimes it seems like they do. I think it's more along the lines of Regan gets it set up and then goes back to steal a little extra sleep before coming in so she can feel like a guest, too."

"That's a good method."

She heads upstairs and I make my way into the kitchen. As promised, there's a fresh pot of coffee waiting and a basket full of various pastries. Bagels stacked on a plate next to the toaster wait for a smear of the thick whipped cream cheese sitting beside them. A distinct spicy smell fills the air and I look around, eventually finding the pot of heavily spiced apple cider warming on the back burner.

I opt for the coffee, promising myself a glass of cider later, and fill a plate with some of the goodies before heading out to the back deck. It's a beautiful morning; it will be nice to sit out there and look out over the lake while I eat. I'm not the only one who had that idea: as soon as I step outside, I see Maya sitting in one of the chaise lounges, a half-eaten bagel on her lap and her hand wrapped around a glass mug of cider. She isn't moving and for a second it looks like a snapshot for a lakeside lodge brochure.

My steps seem to shake her out of her thoughts and she glances back over her shoulder at me.

"Oh, hey, Emma," she greets me.

"Hi," I say. "I see I'm not the only one who thinks this is the perfect spot for breakfast."

"It's one of my favorite things," she says. "I love watching the sunrise over the water. Didn't quite make it this morning, but this is pretty good. Is Bellamy doing OK?"

I sit down on a chair beside her and shrug as I peel off part of my cheese Danish. "She went to sleep pretty much immediately after getting inside. This has all really come down hard on her, especially adding in missing her daughter and feeling almost responsible."

She looks at me quizzically. "Why would she feel responsible? She didn't do anything."

"I think that's the exact reason. She feels like she should have somehow known something was wrong and be able to change it," I say.

"She doesn't have control over everything. People make decisions and sometimes they're bad ones. I hate that it turned out this way, but she shouldn't torture herself over it," she says.

A few moments later, the door opens and Bellamy comes out with Adam close behind. She's holding a cup of coffee close to her chest with one hand and a plate in the other. She perches beside me on the chair and I look into her mug. It's pale and creamy just like she likes it, but doesn't smell as overwhelmingly flavored as usual.

"What do you have?" I ask.

"I taught her a new favorite trick," Adam says.

I look at Bellamy questioningly. "We dissolved marshmallows into our coffee."

"Then added chocolate syrup and cinnamon," Adam adds.

"Wow. That's next level," I note.

"So, what's the plan for today?" Maya asks.

"I guess we're going to do the memorial like Regan was talking about," Adam says.

He doesn't look directly at her and I wonder if that's more about the conversation they had last night or her volunteering him to speak at the memorial.

"I guess we should get ready, then," he says and turns to go back into the house.

Bellamy and I exchange glances, both of us catching the same tension when he turned away.

After breakfast, we get dressed and Regan leads us out onto the floating dock. It's chilly out over the water, but there's also an eeriness hanging over the space that puts a shiver along my spine. I feel bad for feeling that way. This is supposed to be a memorial. It was the entire point of us getting together for the weekend. Maya, Regan, and Priscilla thought it would be a good idea for us all to be together and enjoy some time while also remembering their lost friends.

But this feels heavy and awkward. There was no plan, no preparation, which seems strange considering the attention to detail in the other areas of the weekend. Maybe they couldn't bring themselves to think about it too much. Or maybe it's nothing more than they want to be casual. This was one of the places where they enjoyed just relaxing and spending time together. Having a low-key memorial could be a way to honor that.

I just wish I wasn't here. I feel like an intruder. Like everything that's happening around me is performative. Everybody here is trying to prove something. Or disprove something. They want me to think something specific about who they are and what role they played in the lives of Liza, Finn, and Darren, and what they are to each other.

The only one here I really know is Bellamy, and even she seems different around them. Not in a major way that seems like I don't know her anymore, but just enough that it's like being around this group causes them all to shift to accommodate each other.

"We all know why we're here," Regan starts. "We've lost amazing people and our lives will never be the same. I know I speak for all of us when I say I can't believe they're actually gone. Part of me feels like any second they're just going to show up and apologize for being late. They'll say they got wrapped up in their building project, or that they were binge-watching that awful show he loved but she only tolerated for him." Her head hangs. "I know a lot of things have come to light that we didn't know, but I don't want to think about those things right now.

"All that matters is the people we loved. We knew them. We knew who they were. Even if they had secrets or things they were ashamed of, they were still those people. And that's what I want to think about right now. Is that alright with everyone?"

"I think that's exactly what we should do," Adam takes from her lead. "There's no reason to let anything change the way we remember them. To be honest, we don't even know the whole story. We don't really know what was going on. What we do know is they were our friends. We cared about them and loved them. Each in our own way. Each for our own reasons. But we don't have to change that. They're gone now and nothing is going to make that any different. Trying to make ourselves hate them or not think about them will only hurt us."

"We can't pretend everything is exactly the way it always was," Maya chimes in. "It's not. It won't ever be. I can't ever think of them the same way. It doesn't mean I hate them. But they're different. And it makes me wonder what else I don't know about them."

"Is this really what we're going to talk about?" Priscilla asks. "This is supposed to be a time to remember them and honor them. We're going to spend this time talking about how much their personal lives, things they were purposely keeping to themselves because they didn't want to share them, affects us? It was their marriage. They might have had problems and she might have made a wrong choice in having an affair, but it was her choice. It didn't have anything to do with any of us. How could you stand there and make it about us? Have any of you considered the reason they didn't tell us about what was going on was that they thought we'd manage to make it about ourselves?"

"I can't do this," Adam suddenly says. "I can't stand here and do this anymore."

He jogs up the dock toward the house, ignoring Maya and Bellamy calling after him.

CHAPTER THIRTY-THREE

"I DON'T THINK I CAN DO THIS ANYMORE EITHER," BELLAMY SAYS. "I thought it was a good idea, but it's too hard. And it definitely doesn't feel like a holiday. I can't sit down and pretend it's Thanksgiving and everything is OK."

"Bellamy," Priscilla frowns.

She shakes her head. "I'm sorry. This is just too hard. I miss my baby. I miss Eric. I just feel like we should leave."

She looks over at me like she's asking permission. I immediately nod. This isn't my choice.

"Absolutely. Let's go pack."

My best friend is shuddering as I wrap my arm around her shoulder and guide her back into the house. We go up the stairs into our room and pack. I finish packing and go to Bellamy's room to see if she needs any help. Maya is in there with her, her face in her hands as she sobs.

"Adam left," Bellamy tells me. "His car is gone and he's not answering his phone."

"What's going on with him?" Maya asks. "How could he be acting this way?"

"Maya, is there something we should know? Something you haven't told us?" I ask.

She lifts her head and looks at me through red-rimmed, teary eyes. "What do you mean?"

"I heard the two of you talking last night. It sounds like there's a lot more to your relationship than you're letting on."

"I don't know what you're talking about," she protests. "Darren and I are together. I told you that."

"I know that's what you've been saying. But I heard what you were saying. And I can't help but notice that you have been spending just about all day at the hospital with Darren, but as soon as you come here and you're with Adam, you don't seem to be having a problem not checking on him or are there to take care of him."

"So, I'm not allowed to take a break? I have to devote every second of my life to someone who's already being taken care of by an entire team of doctors and nurses? I guess this is what I get for trying to include a cutthroat FBI agent in my friends," Maya snaps.

"Maya, that's really harsh," Bellamy says.

"Seriously? You think that's harsh? I went out of my way to invite her to come here this weekend because she's important to you. But don't you think that I know who she is?"

"She's the woman who is making sure the investigation into what happened to our friends—people you say you care about—is taken seriously," Bellamy says. "Emma works her ass off and she gets answers when no one else can. You are lucky to have her here and that she is willing to do any of this. She didn't have to take on this investigation. She didn't have to be here or help with the doctor. She could have stayed home and kept working on her other cases. But she came here and has done nothing but help us."

Maya looks like she is going to say something else, then her head drops. She shakes it back and forth.

"I'm sorry. This is just a lot. I don't want you to go. Either of you. This weekend is really important to me and I think we can still salvage it. Can you stay? Please?"

"It would really mean a lot to us," Priscilla adds, walking into the room. "I miss all of us being together. And I know you don't know us as well, Emma, but we heard about you all the time. Bellamy told us stories about you and we saw pictures. I don't know about the others, but I felt like we knew you. I felt like you were kind of a part of us already, or at least that you would be if we met."

She looks over at Maya, who nods. I glance at Bellamy. This still isn't my choice. It has to be Bellamy.

"Alright," she sighs. "We'll stay."

As the words are coming out of her mouth, my phone rings. I see it is Detective Gabriel's number and I pick it up immediately, walking out of the room and into the hallway so I can speak.

"Agent Griffin," I answer.

"Emma, I have some more information for you. That toxicology finally came back."

"Arsenic?"

"Yes, but here's the thing. There wasn't very much."

"What do you mean?"

"The level of arsenic in Liza Fielding's body wasn't high enough to be lethal," he explains.

"That doesn't make sense." I remember what Xavier told me about the Lafarge case. "What samples were checked? Are there others that can be tested? Hair, eyes, stomach? Could you establish if there was long-term exposure?"

"No, but that's the next step of testing."

"Okay. That needs to be done as soon as possible. I'm going to talk to the doctor," I say.

I hang up and go back into the room. "Bellamy, we need to get to the hospital."

"What's going on?" Bellamy raises an eyebrow.

"Is it Darren?" Maya asks.

"Liza's toxicology came back. There was arsenic present."

"Oh, no," Priscilla gasps.

"They need to do additional testing and I want to speak with the doctor about it."

"We'll wait here," Priscilla says.

"What?" Maya says. "I want to go. I need to be with Darren."

"We need to be here when Adam comes back," Priscilla says. "He isn't answering his phone and I don't want to just leave him a voicemail. We need to be here to tell him what's going on."

"She's right," I say. "Stay here. Keep everybody together and I'll let you know as soon as there's any more information."

Bellamy and I jump into the car and head for the hospital.

"There wasn't enough," I tell her.

"What?" Bellamy asks. "What do you mean?"

"There wasn't enough arsenic. The level in Liza's body wasn't enough to be lethal."

"But she died," Bellamy points out. "So did Finn. What about his results?"

"They haven't come back yet, but I'm going to guess there will be the same results."

The extra twenty minutes makes the drive to the hospital feel far too long, and I'm already running by the time I get out of the car. Dr. Kelsey is coming down the hallway when I get out of the elevator and she looks at me with curious eyes.

"Agent Griffin? What's going on?"

"Did you hear from the detectives?" I ask.

"No," she says, shaking her head. "I got a message that someone called and needed to speak with me. I assumed it was you. It might have been them. Why?"

"How is Darren? Has his condition gotten worse?"

"No, actually, he's doing better. We were able to get him awake and have been clearing his system."

"Has he eaten anything?" I ask.

"Only a tray from the hospital."

"Alright. Keep it that way. Has he been able to tell you anything that happened to him?" I ask.

"No. He says he doesn't remember anything about the day he got sick."

"Alright. Do you have time to talk right now?"

"Sure, I can take a few..."

"Adam," Bellamy says.

I look over at the elevator and see Adam coming out of it. He looks agitated and on edge. Tears that streaked down his cheeks have gone without being wiped away, and there's something in his eyes that's a combination of anger, sadness, and pain.

"I want to see Darren," he says as he approaches us. "I don't understand why Maya can see him and none of the rest of us are."

"You can go in," Dr. Kelsey tells him. "He's still dealing with everything, so he might not be awake. But you can talk to him."

"Thank you."

"Adam, wait," I start before he walks away. "I need to ask you something. Is there anything going on between you and Maya?"

"No," he says without hesitation. "Why?"

"I heard the two of you talking last night."

He rolls his eyes. "You heard her talking. In her mind maybe there's something between us, but it's not reality. It hasn't been."

"Okay," I say. "Go ahead."

Adam goes down the hall to Darren's room and the doctor and I go to her office with Bellamy. As soon as we sit down, I tell the doctor what the detectives told me.

"I don't understand," she frowns. "Her symptoms looked like

poison and that seemed to be confirmed by the arsenic showing up in the salt shaker."

"I know. She didn't have any health problems and neither did Finn as far as I know, right, Bellamy?"

She nods. "I mean, as we've found out recently, we don't know everything about each other apparently, but as far as I know, they were both healthy."

"How about Darren?"

"He had high blood pressure," Bellamy shrugs. "But that's it and it wasn't even really serious."

Dr. Kelsey nods. "It's in his chart. He takes medication for it."

Suddenly a light flashes on the corner of her desk. She immediately reaches for her phone.

"Dr. Kelsey," she answers. Her eyes widen. "I'm on my way."

"What's wrong?" I ask, getting to my feet as she rushes for the door.

"There's an emergency call in Darren's room."

We run after her, my heart pounding in my chest. I stop in my tracks when we get to the hallway and I see the swarm of doctors and nurses. They aren't in the room with Darren. They are right outside, tending to a person prone on the floor. It's Adam.

"What the hell is going on?" Bellamy whispers tearfully, her hands clasped over her mouth. "Emma, what the fuck is going on?"

I wish I could answer.

CHAPTER THIRTY-FOUR

"He went into that room and fifteen minutes later, he was on the floor," I tell Detective Gabriel. "He called the nurse's station once complaining of dizziness and a sick stomach, then apparently stumbled out of the room and collapsed."

The detective looks as shocked and bewildered as I feel.

What the hell is going on here?

"What happened just before going to the hospital?" the detective asks.

"We were at the lake house and had breakfast. But that was this morning, and we all ate and drank the same things. None of the rest of us have any symptoms at all. He left the house before you called me. So, maybe he ate or drank something between when he left and when he got there, but the timing seems strange."

"What's happening with Adam now?"

"The doctors are working to save him, but they don't know exactly what's wrong. They're going to administer activated charcoal to absorb any poison he might have ingested. I need you to go back over everything that was found at the Fielding house and Darren's workshop. Every bit of evidence that could possibly mean anything. I need it," I tell him.

"Alright. I'll do what I can."

"Thank you. Bellamy is getting in touch with the others right now. Something is exposing these people to a potentially deadly substance one by one and we need to make sure the rest of them are still safe," I say. "I'll get in touch later."

I walk out of the office and as I'm heading out of the building, Bellamy is running toward me.

"They won't answer their phones," she says.

"None of them?"

She shakes her head. "I tried to call Maya, Regan, and Priscilla, and none of them will answer. The lake house still has a landline because cell service can be unreliable out there. But they didn't answer that, either."

"Come on," I say. "We need to get out there."

We drive back to the house as fast as we can. I'm tense as we step through the front door. Bellamy and I both call out to the other women, but there's no response. We walk through each room and I hear Bellamy let out a cry. Rushing toward the sound of her voice, I find her standing in the kitchen looking down at Regan sprawled out across the tile.

I immediately drop down beside her and press my fingers to her neck, then to her wrist, looking for any sign of a pulse. There is none, and she's not breathing.

"She's dead. We have to find Maya and Priscilla."

We find Maya in a reading room for the back of the house. She's on the floor, curled up in the fetal position. As we move toward her, I notice her head rocking back and forth slightly. She lets out a groan.

"She's alive," Bellamy calls back to me.

"Call for an ambulance. I'm going to look for Priscilla."

I can't find her even after searching all the rooms. I get back to the kitchen where Regan's body is lying and noticed a fresh tray of coffee sitting on the counter. Most of the pot is gone, along with half of the cream. I'm about to walk out of the room when I notice the small bowl of sugar cubes sitting on the tray. My mind goes back to this morning and last night. Both times, the sugar cubes weren't there. The first time, there was raw sugar. The second, Adam and Bellamy melted marshmallows into their mugs.

Bellamy comes into the room and I point out the bowl.

"Sugar cubes," she says.

I nod. "They've been at every scene. Liza and Finn both drink coffee. Remember, Finn drank a tremendous amount of it before he died. They were using coffee Darren roasted, which means it came with a bag of these sugar cubes. And Darren would have them at his workshop. I'm guessing if he includes them with all of the coffee he roasts, it's because it's what he prefers in his own cup."

"What do you think that means? Do you think he killed Liza and Finn, then used the sugarcubes to kill himself?" she asks.

"No, but I think if CSU collected those and sent them to the lab for testing, they'd find arsenic in them," I tell her. "Remember, there wasn't enough in their systems to kill them. They were just exposed to it."

"I don't understand," Bellamy says.

"When I was looking for Priscilla, I went into Regan's room. There was a wet spot on the carpet that looked like coffee. It was really humid in there, like she had just taken a shower, and it seems like she was trying to drink a cup, slipped on her way out of the bathroom and spilled it, then came back in here for another cup."

"I'm getting my stuff," she says. "I need to get out of here."

"Me, too."

We head to our rooms and pack everything. As I start out of the room, I notice a few things have been moved around. It looks like one of the lamps was turned off aggressively and pushed off to the side of the table, and the welcome basket has been turned around. I look through the rest of the room and see a couple of small changes, but nothing significant. It looks like someone came into the room to look for something but tried not to be detected.

Bellamy and I wait outside for the police to arrive. I introduce myself to the uniformed officers I don't know and catch Detective Gabriel up on what's happening. Because we can prove the women were alive when we left the house and that we were at the hospital when they got sick, the police agree to let Bellamy and me go check into a hotel rather than making us stay at the scene or go to the precinct to make a statement.

Once we're there, she falls apart. She rocks back and forth on the edge of the bed, her fingers digging in her hair as she tries to understand what's going on.

"This doesn't make any sense, Emma. First we think it's a natural death, that Liza just got sick and died. Then, it looked like murder and her husband committed suicide because of it. It seems like arsenic and it looks like we're making some progress, but then… what? They consumed arsenic but it didn't hurt them? They're dead for no reason? And now the others? I don't understand."

"The toxicology reports from Finn and the tests done on Darren and Adam are going to come back with arsenic exposure," I say. "I can guarantee the women will, as well. And the sugar cubes will be contaminated. There was arsenic in the salt shaker at the Fielding house, but I am positive those sugar cubes were also poisoned.

"Other investigators would say it's clear Darren is the one who was having an affair with Liza. He killed the others with the poisoned sugar, but couldn't handle the guilt and ended up killing himself. He did it for revenge and out of sadness and anger at being humiliated."

"It makes sense," Bellamy nods.

"But it doesn't. It's too neat. It's too convenient. And the levels of arsenic are not lethal. These people consumed arsenic but it did not kill them. Something else got to each one of them one by one, so what was it?"

"And what about Adam?" she asks.

"Exactly," I say. "He wasn't even around to have the sugar cubes. But he collapsed at the hospital. How did he get sick?"

"I don't even know what to do."

"I need to talk to the police again," I say.

"About what?" she asks. "What are you thinking?"

"I'm not sure yet. You need to go to the hospital and keep an eye on Maya, Adam, and Darren. Keep trying to get in touch with Priscilla. I'll get in touch with you as soon as I can."

CHAPTER THIRTY-FIVE

"But there was no arsenic in her body," Detective Gabriel says. "The toxicology did not find any, and they did an extensive analysis. Her hair, her eyes, her liver, everything. There was nothing."

"That's what I'm trying to explain to you. The arsenic is not what caused these deaths and illnesses. It's a cover-up."

"A cover-up?"

"Yes," I confirm. "I don't know why, but someone put arsenic in that salt and in the sugar cubes so that it would be found. They wanted it to be identified. Whoever is causing this wanted people to think it was arsenic. They intended everyone exposed to die from the exposure and for it to be classified as being arsenic poisoning. They were setting someone up to look like the murderer."

"But what is it about Cheryl Bishop's death that caught your attention?"

"It has many of the same hallmarks. She was a very healthy woman. She died with the same symptoms very suddenly," I explain. "It might just be a coincidence, but I need to look into it more."

"It is a strange coincidence," Detective Gabriel admits.

"That's just the thing. I don't believe in coincidence. People don't just die like this, not one after another."

"No, I mean, the vaping. Super healthy, but vaped. A ton of nicotine was apparently in her system. That doesn't go together."

I pause. "No, it doesn't. That's not a habit I would expect her to have."

The detective goes to the evidence locker and brings back everything they collected, including Cheryl's phone. I don't have a search warrant and I don't want to waste the time to try to get one that could potentially get turned down, so I take a leap. Using the personal information the police have about Cheryl, I get in touch with her mother. As her next of kin, she can authorize me to look through the phone.

"Of course," Mrs. Bishop tells me once I explain the situation. "If you think it might help you find out what happened to her."

"It might," I say. "Thank you very much. I appreciate you doing this."

"Thank you for caring enough to try to find out what happened to my Cheryl."

"Can I ask you one more thing?" I ask before she hangs up.

"What is it?"

"How long did your daughter have a vaping habit?" I ask.

There's a moment of silence through the phone. "Vaping habit?"

"Yes. Electronic cigarettes," I explain.

"I know what it is," she says. "I'm just confused. Cheryl would never do something like that."

"Oh," I say. "I'm sorry, it's just that there was evidence of heavy nicotine use in her autopsy."

"No. There must have been some sort of mistake. She was very outspoken about how much she disagreed with things like that. She never would have done it."

"Okay. Thank you, again."

I get off the phone and immediately reach for Cheryl's. It has already been unlocked by the detectives doing her initial investigation, so I'm able to go through it. The first thing I do is look at her contacts and it doesn't take long for something to stand out.

∽

"Liza's phone number was in Cheryl Bishop's phone," I tell Bellamy over speakerphone as I drive back to the hospital.

"Cheryl Bishop, the woman who died a few weeks ago?" she asks.

"That would be her. And when I looked through her text messages, I found one from Liza with a tracking number in it."

"Oh, my gosh, she must have been a customer. She ordered from Liza's company."

"Liza and Maya's company," I point out.

When I get back to the hospital, Bellamy and I go into the room where Maya is stretched out in the bed, hooked up to an IV and looking worn and tired. But at least fully conscious and alive.

"How are you feeling?" Bellamy asks. "You look better."

"Horrible," she says. "They treated me with activated charcoal. It might have saved my life, but I feel awful. How is Adam?"

"He's alive," I say. "But I need you to be honest with us now."

She looks down at her legs and starts to cry. "I'm sorry. I'm sorry I lied to you before. You did hear us talking." She looks up at me. "Adam and I were in love. We've been together for a long time and had started talking about getting married. We haven't said anything to anybody because we have such a history and knew it would cause a lot of drama. Then there's Darren and I hadn't figured out how to break things off with him. I was just about to when all this happened. I feel so guilty for cheating on him. But at the same time, I felt like it was justified considering what he was doing."

"What do you mean?" I ask.

"His affair with Liza," she continues. "Adam and I were going through a rough patch when Darren and I started seeing each other. I found out he was having an affair with Liza and was devastated, but he insisted things were over between the two of them. If either one of us had just been upfront and honest, none of this would have happened."

"You acted so surprised when we found Liza's journals and saw she was having an affair," Bellamy points out.

"Because I was embarrassed. And I didn't want anyone to know what was happening between me and Darren, or me and Adam."

"Here's the thing, Maya. We talked to Adam about the two of you."

"You did?"

"Yes, and he said nothing was going on," I say.

"I'm not surprised he would say that. I told you we were trying to keep it quiet," Maya sighs. "He didn't want to hurt anyone."

"Right now, there are people far more than hurt and I think he understands that."

"He was trying to protect himself," Maya says, slightly shifting her approach. "He wanted to protect his reputation. He just didn't know we weren't going to be able to keep our secret for long."

"What do you mean? Why not?" I ask.

"I'm pregnant and it's Adam's. I didn't even get a chance to tell him yet. Now I'm so worried the baby is going to be hurt by whatever made us all so sick."

I'm baffled by what I'm hearing. I don't even know what to say.

"You didn't know Cheryl?" I ask Bellamy later.

"No," she shakes her head. "I've never heard of her."

"It's too much of a coincidence. I need to find out what happened to her house. If it hasn't been cleared out yet, maybe there's a way to find more evidence. I just don't know what to look for."

We spend the evening in tense silence, still trying to get ahold of Priscilla with no luck. I call Sam and update him, and he reports back that he has nothing much to report back from his investigation.

The night is tense, but we eventually drift off.

We're woken up by the ringing of Bellamy's phone. It's a call from Adam, and in an instant, we're on our way to the hospital again. Adam meets us in the hallway, sitting on a bench with his head in his hands.

"Darren is dead," he says.

Bellamy looks like her knees are going to buckle.

"What happened?" I ask. "He was doing better."

"I don't know. The doctors just said that the poison must have done so much damage to his body it just couldn't recover," he says.

"Adam, I know this is a horrible moment to do this, but we can't waste any more time. I'm going to ask you something again and I need you to be completely honest with me."

"Alright," he says.

"Are you or have you recently been sleeping with Maya?"

"No," he says insistently.

"Not at all?" I ask.

"Absolutely not. I told you, she makes up things. She's been obsessed with me since we first went out on a couple of dates years and years ago. I haven't had anything to do with her other than our interactions with the rest of the friends in years."

"Then how is she pregnant with your child?"

His face goes blank. "Excuse me?"

"She's pregnant, Adam. And she says it's yours."

"She's lying. I haven't had sex with her. She can't be pregnant, at least not with my baby. I want a paternity test," he says.

"Has anyone notified Maya of Darren's death?" I ask.

"No," Adam says. "She was released this morning and has been in the chapel since. I haven't spoken to her."

"Then let's go talk to her," I say.

"Emma," Bellamy protests.

"We can't waste this time," I say. "We need to find out what's going on. Confronting her about the pregnancy might help us do that."

CHAPTER THIRTY-SIX

We leave Maya sobbing, but I can't bring myself to feel bad for her. I'm numb. I don't understand what's going on and there are too many issues coming from all directions for me to choose one and feel much of anything for it.

When Adam confronted her about the baby, she dissolved, going into hysterics because he was denying her even when he knew there was a baby involved. Adam continued to be insistent that there was nothing between them, even when she was able to present documentation that she is, in fact, pregnant.

The only way to do a paternity test is with an amniocentesis, but the invasive test is painful and can be very dangerous to the baby. Maya refuses to have one, saying Adam can just wait until the baby is born to find out the truth. She's not going to risk the baby's life just to prove what she already knows.

I don't know if this makes me believe her more or less. She could be telling the truth and Adam is just digging in his heels to avoid having to deal with it. Or she could be lying and is trying to seem more believable with the refusal in the hope she will be moved by it and accept it without proof.

With nothing else to go on, I go back to the hotel and to the beginning.

Xavier's lecture about arsenic was fascinating, I'll give him that, but it didn't give me all the details. It was enough, however, to spark my research. The theory of it being the murder weapon is officially debunked for me. There was simply too little in their systems and it killed too fast. A person needs to build up toxicity over time to die from arsenic poisoning.

Suddenly, something catches my attention.

"Bellamy," I call.

She comes over to me, sitting on the bed and leaning her head back against the wall.

"Hmm?"

"Didn't you say that Adam was sick pretty recently? Or he had an infection? Something?"

"He got hurt while he was working on the deck. It was a pretty nasty cut on his leg."

"Did he have to get stitches?" I ask.

"I think five or six," she nods.

"So, the doctor would have put him on antibiotics?" I ask.

"Yes. He was complaining about them because he hates how antibiotics make him feel. Why?"

"I'm reading about poisons, and this says that there are accepted amounts of substances that are considered lethal and amounts of time it generally takes for them to be processed by the body and cause damage. But many factors influence this, including taking medications. Certain medications change the speed of metabolism of substances. Some speed it up and some slow it down. Antibiotics speed it up. High blood pressure medications slow it down."

"Like Darren."

"Exactly. Adam got sick a lot faster than the others, and Darren was able to just hang on. Whatever they had in their system was affected by their medications."

Her phone alerts on the table and she picks it up.

"Oh, god," she gasps.

"What is it?"

"Maya miscarried the baby."

Maya is sobbing in her bed when we get back to the hospital. I feel like I've driven that drive and walked through those doors a thousand times at this point. I don't want to do it again. I want this to be over.

"I can't believe it's gone," she whispers. "My baby is gone."

"I'm so sorry," Bellamy says.

"It's the stress," she says. "The stress of all this happening killed my baby."

"Did you have a paternity test performed?" I ask.

"Emma!" Bellamy snaps.

"It would be easy to do," I point out. "Both of them were agreeable for after the baby was born. Now is the time. I'm sorry to be crass or to seem insensitive. I am very sorry for your loss. But this is important."

"Emma, right now isn't the time."

"Yes, it is," Maya says.

"What?" Bellamy asks.

"There's not going to be another time," Maya says. "This is the only time when there is going to be a chance for this to get done. I need Adam to know this is the truth. I need him to admit to it. Maybe there's still a chance we could be together."

The test is fast and less than an hour later, we're standing with Adam as he shakes his head in disbelief.

"It can't be mine," he mutters. "I don't know what to tell you, but it can't be mine."

"There's no way for you to deny it," I tell him. "The test results are right there. That baby has your DNA. It's yours."

"But I haven't been sleeping with Maya. I wouldn't," he says.

"You have before," I say.

"Yes, years ago. But not now. Not with Liza," he says.

The words hit me in the gut.

"With Liza?" I ask. "What do you mean? I thought Darren was having the affair with her."

He takes a shaky breath and nods. "It was me," he says. "I'm the one she was having an affair with. It's been going on for a couple of years and I was completely in love with her. It killed me every day to see her with Finn. I knew we should be together. But she wouldn't leave him. Not yet, anyway."

"What did you do?" I ask.

"I didn't kill her," he says. "I would never hurt her. Not for a second. That's why I dealt with her staying married to him. She said going through a divorce would be complicated and expensive, and it could be detrimental to her career. She wasn't ready to go through all of that yet. But over the last few months, she had started to change her mind. It was really hard for her because Finn was good to her. Everything we said about their relationship was true. He doted on her. He was kind to her."

"Then why did she cheat on him?" I ask.

"Has anyone ever been kind to you in hopes that you would fall in love with them, but you couldn't?" he asks.

That question hits hard. I simply nod, the image of Greg's face coming into my mind, but his name stays off my lips. I don't want to put that out into the world. There's no need.

"Why didn't you say anything about this earlier?" I ask. "When she was first killed, why didn't you say anything?"

"When she first died, I thought it was natural causes. That she got sick or had an infection. For a while, even though it might be my fault because I was taking those antibiotics and she was allergic to some of them. But it didn't seem like an allergic reaction that killed her. Then when Finn died, I got scared. Them both dying that way made it look like I had done it. Anybody knew she was having an affair with me, they would think I killed him out of jealousy."

"You still look guilty," I point out. "It still looks like you did all of this."

"I know," he admits. "But I didn't. And I will do anything I need to do to prove it."

I believe him. I don't know why and none of this makes sense anymore, but I believe him. But what I don't believe is that he doesn't have anything to do with Maya. The proof is right there. She was pregnant with his child, and the conversation we were having at the lake house tells me there's more to this story. Whether he loved Liza or not, there's more.

"What are you going to do now?" Bellamy asks when we leave Adam.

"I need to look over the security camera footage from Darren's room. I had that camera installed so that it could be monitored to make sure he was kept safe. But everybody who watched it said nothing ever happened in there. He was never given any outside food or drink. Nobody ever messed with his IVs. It doesn't seem possible that anything could have happened. But that's why I need to look at it. Maybe I'll notice something they don't," I say.

It doesn't take long for them to produce the footage from the camera. We scan through day after day. It's exactly what we already know happened. The doctors and nurses come in and tend to him. Take his vitals. Make sure he's doing all right. Maya comes in and sits with them, reading to him, talking to him. She brushes his hair and puts the lotion on his skin.

Then it comes to the day of Adam's collapse. We watch him go into the room and talk to Darren for a few seconds. He looks worked up and

I can only admit that his behavior points more and more like he's the one responsible for all this. At one point, he looks down at his hands and rubs them together like they feel dry. I know that feeling. Winter air can be detrimental to its skin. He picks up a tube of lotion next to the bed and rubs some into his skin.

He continues to talk, but it's only a few minutes later when he visibly starts to feel ill. He rubs his stomach and his head. He covers his mouth with his hand. He reaches out to grab the nurse call button and says something into the intercom. A few seconds later, he stands and stumbles across the room. I know that's when he went out into the hallway and collapsed.

"Nothing happened," Bellamy frowns. "We just watched all of it and nothing happened."

"Wait," I tell her. "Scroll it back. Let me watch Maya in there again."

We are going through the footage again and I squint to pay as close attention to the footage as possible. My eyes are tired and don't want to focus, but I force them to anyway.

"She just takes care of him," Bellamy says. "Which really makes me mad now that I know what was going on."

"But look how she taking care of him," I point. "She tucks the blankets around him, brushes his hair, touches his face, kisses him. All of that. But then when she picks up the lotion to put it on his skin, she put gloves on. Why would you put gloves on?"

"Nurses usually put gloves on when they're washing a patient or applying lotion," Bellamy offers. "Remember, she was a nurse first. It might just be an impulse."

"Maybe," I say. "But he's not a patient or her. She's supposed to care for this man. He's supposed to be her boyfriend. And she's able to touch him all the other times, but suddenly when it comes to applying lotion, she has to put on gloves?"

I go out to the nurse's station and ask about the lotion. I find out there are tubes in every room. The air in hospitals can be so dry and often patients experience cracks that can get infected. They're encouraged to keep their hands and feet, in particular, moisturized. I ask one of the nurses to come with me to look at the footage and point out the bottle Maya is using.

"Yes," she confirms. "That looks like the lotion we provide patients. Here, I can show you a bottle."

She comes back a few seconds later with another bottle of lotion. It looks exactly like the kind Maya is holding in the video. I thank her and she goes back to the station. But moments later, another nurse comes into the room.

"You were asking about the lotion that the woman put on that patient Darren O'Malley who just died?" she asks.

"Yes," I nod. "But it looks like it was just the lotion that the hospital provides to everybody."

"That's right," she says. "She always used a bottle that was sitting by the bed. But I noticed whenever I came in either while she was putting it on or right after, it smelled different in the room."

"It smelled different?" I repeat.

"Yes," she says. "The lotion from the hospital is unscented. Fragrances can trigger allergic reactions and other issues on sensitive skin. They're just not necessary in a therapeutic setting. But when she put lotion on him, there was always a scent in the air. I couldn't really identify it, and I thought maybe it was her perfume."

"What did it smell like?" Bellamy asks.

"It's really hard to describe," she says.

"Sweet?" I offer. "Maybe a little like black pepper?"

"Exactly," the nurse says, her eyes opening wide. "That's what it smelled like."

"Thank you so much."

CHAPTER THIRTY-SEVEN

"Do you still have any of the stuff from that welcome basket at the lake house?" I ask Bellamy.

"Yeah, I packed it in my stuff. I was going to bring it home and take a bubble bath because I never got a chance to while I was there."

"Don't open it. I need you to go to the hotel, get them out, and take pictures of them. Every bottle, okay?"

"Kay. Where are you going?"

"The police station," I tell her. "I need to look over Cheryl's crime scene photos again."

It takes almost half an hour for Bellamy to get back to the hotel and send me the pictures. During that same time, I pull out the pictures from Cheryl's files and also look up pictures on the social media accounts of all of the victims. I have them lined up across my screen and the table, ready for comparison.

When she sends the picture, something goes off in my head. I dig out the toxicology reports for each of the victims that we've gotten back. Seconds later, I have Detective Gabriel in the room with me.

"We need more testing done," I tell him.

"For what?" he raises an eyebrow.

"Nicotine levels," I say.

"Nicotine?" he asks. "Why would we check for that?"

"It isn't done on just basic autopsy reports or toxicology. It has to be looked for specifically because you can't find just nicotine. Instead, you find breakdown materials. And those breakdown materials could be present for any number of reasons, but generally because a person is a smoker. Or a vaper. When we were talking about Cheryl Bishop, you mentioned how strange it was that she lives such a healthy lifestyle, but vaped.

"However, I spoke to her mother and she said we never would have used electronic cigarettes. Ever. She was always very outspoken about the use of tobacco and never would have done it. Which means that those breakdown materials that showed up on the toxicology report because of her suspicious death came from something else," I explain.

"Were the levels in Cheryl Bishop's report high?"

"Yes," I nod. "But it's not that unusual for something like that to show up and not be a cause for alarm. It's actually like arsenic, dictating build-up in the system. People who are longtime smokers or users of other tobacco products will have traces of nicotine in their tissues for a long time after they quit using it. It shows up in their hair, their eyes, their tissues. Everywhere. And there's a massive controversy about how much is actually lethal. So even when the amounts seem very high, they might not pay attention to them because there is a belief that people can actually be exposed to a huge amount of nicotine and be fine."

"I'll get those tests ordered."

"Nicotine poisoning?" Bellamy asks later as we make our way to Maya's house.

"Yes," I say. "You need to get in touch with Priscilla and make sure she didn't use any of those products."

It was a relief when Bellamy got a text saying that Priscilla had gotten into an argument with Maya and decided to leave soon after Adam did. She'd gone off on her own for a little while, disconnecting from everyone. It left what felt like a terrifying dangling thread in the investigation, but I'm glad it's finally fixed.

"I will," she says. "But I don't think I understand."

"Don't worry," I say. "You will soon."

Maya meets us at the door in a sweatsuit. She still looks distraught and a piece deep inside me feels bad for her. I know she is going through genuine pain. Whatever happened and whatever she has done, she is still suffering one of the worst types of pain a woman can go through. But I can only give myself a few moments to have that compassion. Now I need to get back to why I'm here.

And that's the victims.

"How are you holding up?" I ask.

"About as well as you expect me to," she says. "I lost my baby and the love of my life. I'm choosing to, with all of my heart, still believe he'll come back to me. We're meant to be together. We always have been."

"Is that why you were so angry when you found out he was having an affair with Liza?" I ask.

"Liza?" she asks, looking confused. "No. Adam wasn't having an affair with her. That was Darren."

"No, Maya. That was Adam. Remember? He told us all about it. That there was no way he had anything going on with you because he was in love with Liza. She and Finn had fallen out of love, and she was going to ask for a divorce so that she could be with Adam."

Maya shakes her head. "No. That wasn't what was happening."

"Yes, it was. It must have been especially painful because she was such a good friend of yours."

"My best friend," Maya whispers. "And she's dead. Please don't forget that."

"Trust me, I haven't. Tell me about your business with her."

"What do you want to know?" she asks.

"How did you decide to go from being a nurse to making welcome baskets? That seems like a very strange career change."

"Making things like soap and lotions was a hobby of mine. I introduced Liza to it, and she thought it was a lot of fun. Then she said maybe we could make some money out of it. I love nursing, but I felt like there was so much more that I could do. We just wanted to do something fun and brighten up people's days. So we came up with different fragrances and products and started advertising them."

"And you had gotten pretty popular, hadn't you?" I ask.

"We were getting there," she says. "There were even a few celebrities who ordered from us."

"That's exciting," I note. "You mentioned that the fragrance you gave us in our welcome bag, was that one the that's your best seller?"

"Yes," she nods.

"And it was one that Liza came up with?" I ask.

"Yes," she says.

Bellamy shakes her head. "No, it wasn't. You came up with that one. You started making the vanilla bourbon scent before Liza got involved."

"See, that's what I thought," I say. "I noticed that Bellamy smelled different when I hugged her one day. I know that sounds weird, but when you've been best friends with somebody for as long as Bellamy and I have, you start to notice things about them. Like the fact that she is always wearing the same scent. When I asked her about it, she said that she had run out of her favorite and so she was using one of yours.

"At the time, I didn't know about your business. So, I just thought you meant that she had borrowed something from you. But what she actually meant was it was sent from your company. One that you created. And because you created it, you knew about the tobacco fragrance profile. You told me about it, remember? And you were right. It is very popular. It has a spicy, warm kind of scent that pairs extremely well with sweet scents like vanilla.

"But it wasn't just the smell of vanilla that was useful for you. See, liquid nicotine isn't all that difficult to find. I'm sure a lot of people have images of having to unwrap tons of cigarettes and soak them in their bathtubs to get it, but actually, they can just go online and buy massive quantities of it. And every single bottle comes with the same warning. Not to let it touch your skin. That is because it soaks through and can be lethal.

"What it also does is turn a faint shade brown when exposed to oxygen. Anyone who has ever worked with high-quality ingredients for body products knows that vanilla does the same thing. So, slipping liquid nicotine, which as you probably figured out by now has the same smell as tobacco because it's distilled from it, into a product already containing vanilla, won't change its appearance."

"That's all fascinating," Maya says, "but everyone was poisoned with arsenic. It's right there on their reports."

"It is," I nod. "And I'm sure when yours comes back, it'll show up there too. Maybe even on the test performed on the baby you lost. But here's the thing. There wasn't nearly enough. None of the victims had anywhere near a lethal dose of arsenic. It wasn't what killed them."

I pause for a moment, watching the emotion roll through Maya's eyes, but she says nothing.

"That arsenic was planted," I go on. "You wanted people to find it and think that's why your friends died. Arsenic and nicotine poisoning have extremely similar symptoms. It can be difficult to tell the difference between them. But if a person died of arsenic poisoning, there will be signs of it in their hair and their tissues. Not just in their stomach. Everybody was exposed to arsenic. Except for Cheryl Bishop."

"Who?" she asks.

"Your client," I say. "The customer who ordered from you. Liza is the one who interacted with her. I bet she wouldn't have if she knew she was participating in an experiment to see if nicotine could really kill when put in bubble bath. Because that's exactly what you did. The candles, the bath salts, the soaps. Those are all safe. But the bubble bath had a strong dose of liquid nicotine so that when it was poured into water and sank down into it, it would seep right through their skin. The exception was for the men. They got poisoned lotion. I noticed you put gloves on before you applied lotion to Darren. And when Adam went to visit him, he put some on.

"The different onset of symptoms was confusing, but it turns out both men were on different types of medication that changed the metabolism of the nicotine in their systems. You didn't prepare for that."

"This is ridiculous," Maya scoffs. "I'm mourning the loss of two friends, my boyfriend, and my baby, and dealing with the man I thought I would marry leaving me. And you're going to come at me with this? Something so absurd? This, Bellamy. This is what I was talking about when I said she was a cutthroat agent."

"Yes," Bellamy says. "Yes, she is."

A tear slides down her cheek as the door opens behind us and the police come in.

EPILOGUE

The smell of Thanksgiving dinner is still in the air, and I have gained approximately thirty pounds in turkey and pumpkin pie, which means that as I lie on Sam's chest and try not to move, Xavier is in his room changing into his Christmas pajamas. There's already a bottle of eggnog in the refrigerator and soon there will be an army of Gingerbread Men of the World in the oven.

"I still don't understand," Sam says. "What about the baby?"

"Do we really have to talk about this right now?" Dean groans. His arm is held over his eyes and bits of spilled gravy are rapidly drying on his sweater. "I thought Thanksgiving was a safe space for disturbing murder talk."

"Well, according to Xavier we are in the transition between Thanksgiving and Christmas, so if she talks fast, she can explain it without defiling either holiday," Sam offers. "I thought Adam wasn't sleeping with Maya."

"Fortunately, it's a fast explanation," I say. "He wasn't."

"What?" Sam asks.

"Remember that Maya was a nurse? Her friends didn't know she was still nursing part-time. At a fertility clinic. It turns out that Finn wasn't the only one making, er... deposits at the bank back in college."

Sam shudders and holds me close. Xavier comes into the room and announces that the holidays have officially changed. I'm fine with that. I'm ready to be done with this and help Bellamy heal. She's coping well and I know things will be hard, but we'll get her through. We're family.

*

One week later ...

"I need to go back to Michigan," Sam tells me, coming into the kitchen with fire in his eyes.

"I thought you were going back in a couple weeks," I frown.

"That was the plan, but I just got a call from the department I'm working with there," he says. "Do you remember Gerald Collins? Rocky?"

"He was the name you found in Marie's phone, right?"

Sam nods.

"He was found dead in his cell this morning."

AUTHOR'S NOTE

Dear Reader,

I hope you enjoyed *The Girl and the Midnight Murder*, book 2 in season 3. Thank you for your continued support with the Emma Griffin series, I hope you continue to love it as much as I love writing it! If you can please continue to leave your reviews for these books, I would appreciate that enormously.

Your reviews allow me to get the validation I need to keep going as an indie author. Just a moment of your time is all that is needed.

My promise to you is to always do my best to bring you thrilling adventures. I can't wait for you to read the books I have in store for you this holiday season!

Yours,
A.J. Rivers

P.S. If for some reason you didn't like this book or found typos or other errors, please let me know personally. I do my best to read and respond to every email at aj@riversthrillers.com

ALSO BY
A.J. RIVERS

Emma Griffin FBI Mysteries by AJ Rivers

Season One
Book One—The Girl in Cabin 13*
Book Two—The Girl Who Vanished*
Book Three—The Girl in the Manor*
Book Four—The Girl Next Door*
Book Five—The Girl and the Deadly Express*
Book Six—The Girl and the Hunt*
Book Seven—The Girl and the Deadly End*

Season Two
Book Eight—The Girl in Dangerous Waters*
Book Nine—The Girl and Secret Society*
Book Ten—The Girl and the Field of Bones*
Book Eleven—The Girl and the Black Christmas*
Book Twelve—The Girl and the Cursed Lake*
Book Thirteen—The Girl and The Unlucky 13*
Book Fourteen—The Girl and the Dragon's Island*

Season Three
Book Fifteen—The Girl in the Woods*
Book Sixteen—The Girl and the Midnight Murder

Other Standalone Novels
Gone Woman*

* Also available in audio

Made in the USA
Columbia, SC
02 March 2022